BENEATH
THE BONFIRE

———

ALSO BY NICKOLAS BUTLER

Shotgun Lovesongs

BENEATH THE BONFIRE

Stories

NICKOLAS BUTLER

THOMAS DUNNE BOOKS ⚏ ST. MARTIN'S PRESS

NEW YORK

THOMAS DUNNE BOOKS.
An imprint of St. Martin's Press.

BENEATH THE BONFIRE. Copyright © 2015 by Nickolas Butler. All rights reserved. Printed in the United States of America. For information, address St. Martin's Press, 175 Fifth Avenue, New York, N.Y. 10010.

www.thomasdunnebooks.com
www.stmartins.com

"Apples" first appeared in *Ploughshares;* "Beneath the Bonfire," originally titled "Underneath the Bonfire," and "Leftovers" first appeared in *Narrative Magazine;* and "The Chainsaw Soirée" first appeared in *The Kenyon Review Online.* Those stories appear here with slight modifications. Special thanks to the editors of the aforementioned journals, in particular DeWitt Henry and Tom Jenks.

Designed by Steven Seighman

The Library of Congress Cataloging-in-Publication Data is available upon request.

ISBN 978-1-250-03983-5 (hardcover)
ISBN 978-1-4668-7553-1 (e-book)

St. Martin's Press books may be purchased for educational, business, or promotional use. For information on bulk purchases, please contact the Macmillan Corporate and Premium Sales Department at 1-800-221-7945, extension 5442, or write to specialmarkets@macmillan.com.

First Edition: May 2015

10 9 8 7 6 5 4 3 2 1

*

For Kristin Carol (Lang) Guice
1980–2014
Beloved cousin and friend. She of belly laughter and wide,
wide Minnesota smiles.

*

And for Carol and George, who took us in when we
needed a home.

CONTENTS

The Good Book says the meek shall inherit the earth and I expect that's probably the truth. I ain't no freethinker, but I'll tell you what. I'm a long way from bein' convinced that it's all that good a thing.

—Cormac McCarthy, *All the Pretty Horses*

BENEATH
THE BONFIRE

———————

THE CHAINSAW SOIRÉE

THEY SQUATTED IN AN ABANDONED Pentecostal church
high on the bluffs over a river, and when the rain or snow
was heavy, the roof leaked and the church was loud with the
dripping of water in metal buckets, and when the land was
dry beneath the floorboards of the church, hundreds of
rattlesnakes shook their maracas at the heat and only at
night would the place fall into silence. I had visited sometimes in the spring when the snakes were lethargic and hungry for the sunlight, and we had stood around the church
with machetes and rakes and turned the yellow grass red.
It was a beautiful spot.

The church was derelict, but their gardens covered acres
of land, radiating off in every direction away from the old
house of worship. Hitchhikers and wandering hippies knew
of Bear and Luna and the church with holes in the roof, and
they came to work and camp on the grounds for free meals

and camaraderie. But I knew Bear from high school. We always dated the same girls.

They threw parties on the winter solstice every year. They called them *chainsaw parties*. Everyone brought a chainsaw, and that was how they built up enough firewood to heat the drafty church all the way through winter. We all went out into the woods early in the morning with flasks of brandy or whiskey and cut up the deadfall or the widow-makers hung up in other living trees. We used sleds to bring the wood back to the church. There were stations around the church: those who split the deadfall into cordwood, those who transported the split wood to other piles, and those who stacked the wood into cords of tight walls. On the solstice, the sun seemed too heavy an object to rise above the earth, but during those rare hours of light, we worked hard, sweating through our layers of garments, the noise of chainsaws everywhere. And afterward, there was a pig roast and a keg of beer and a bonfire and always a guitar or a harmonica and the sad reedy voice of a skinny stoner girl singing to the stars.

The last chainsaw party I attended was years ago, before Shelly and I were married and before Samuel came. I was dating a nurse then, Nancy. She worked at the hospital in neonatal. She had thick blond hair she kept in a braid behind her head, and she smelled of baby powder and soap and I think that I was in love with her. I liked asking Nancy about her work. She would tell me about the babies that had been born that day. The twins, the triplets, the rare hermaphrodite, the stillborn, the beautiful, the already crippled. She rolled her own cigarettes, and I remember her now, sitting in just a T-shirt at my kitchen table, her legs naked and well muscled and folded beneath her on a chair. Her fingers rolling out dozens of cigarettes and sometimes joints. In the morning before she left for work, her hair not yet braided, and it held the light of the sun like fiber-optic cables.

I drove a pickup truck back then. An old Toyota with a rusting bed. I had jacked up the body during high school and removed the bumpers, replacing them with thick black pipes. We left for the church before dawn, Nancy and I in the dusty cab with a thermos of coffee and my old Husqvarna chainsaw in the back. We smoked cigarettes as we drove, the windows cracked open to the cold while the heater blasted out hot air.

She often went down on me while I drove, and her blond head would bob in my lap as I tried to keep my eyes open and the truck between the yellow lines. I remember that morning, the taste of her kiss and the sun rising over the hills and draws. Nancy liked sex, and my life with her was often an exhibition of love, though I could never keep up with her and somewhere along the line I knew that would end us. We made love in the hospital freight elevators and on the helicopter pad on the top of the tall building and once in the basement morgue, where we had stopped prematurely because I thought I heard a sound in all the dead stillness.

"So what's Luna like?" she asked, moving back across the bench seat of the pickup truck as she unscrewed the silver top of the thermos, steam clouding the passenger-side window.

That hadn't always been her name, Luna. Back when her name was Shelly we had been lovers, but Bear had stolen her from me, though of course I know now that it wasn't like that, a theft. That lovers are not just stolen, but that there was something else, like a yielding or an acquiescence. And I had known then that I wasn't wild enough for her, that we were not a permanent thing but rather something more ephemeral. I decided to tell Nancy the truth.

"Luna and I used to date," I said, looking straight out at the road disappearing underneath us. "We dated for two years in high school. Back then, her name was Shelly. She and Bear had a renaming ceremony or some such of a thing." I paused, then, "We were just kid stuff."

"When were you planning to tell me that?" Nancy asked, crossing her arms.

"I just did," I said.

"So, why did you break up?" she asked, her voice sharp.

"She started in with Bear," I said evenly. "I walked in on them one day."

She was quiet, sipping her coffee, drawing stick figures in the condensation on the window. Nancy had beautiful fingers, and I never tired of holding her hands or watching her fingers cradle a mug or a wineglass. Her perfect nails, the long strong fingers.

"People can be terrible to one another," she said finally. And then she leaned against me on the bench seat, her head on my shoulder, and she passed me the coffee and we were still many miles from the church and it felt good to drive that way, her body drawn close against mine as the countryside clipped past us—hawks on the telephone poles, frozen rivers moving invisibly beneath cloaks of ice, horses standing somberly in the fields.

I rarely saw Bear after high school. Just those chainsaw parties and sometimes in the spring when the maple sap was running and he needed an extra pair of hands boiling the syrup down. Things went better between us when there was work to be done and afterward over beers, or sharing a joint when we could talk about the labor and not old times, because I had no interest in the past anymore, or thought I didn't, though we were still in each other's lives somehow, and Luna too.

The church was tall and white, and atop the bluffs it seemed like an impossible outpost of God. There were dogs in the yard, barking at our approach, and in the air hung the smell of woodsmoke and I remember that Nancy closed her door and closed her eyes too and said happily, "I feel happy already. I like this place."

We held hands and approached the great double doors of the church, and just then Bear opened them in tandem and stood before us, his beard long and black, his eyes sparkling blue and the color in his cheeks bright from laboring outdoors. I felt Nancy's grip on my hand slacken.

I introduced Bear and Nancy, and we went into the church. It was warmer than I remembered, with the smell of coffee and of sweat and of dogs, and woodsmoke and to-bacco. Luna was at the sink washing a collection of beets, and her hands looked older than her face, her nails broken and short, but she raised her head and said hello and by and by she came over and hugged us gingerly and it wasn't until she walked back to the sink that I could see from her gait that she was pregnant.

Bear was smiling at me and he said, "Five months along! You believe that? Me, a father!" He slapped my shoulder and my back and I shook his hand again, and he said, "How about a morning toast? Something to keep us warm before we start cutting?"

"That sounds great, man," I said. "Congratulations. Nancy works in the nursery at the hospital, you know, if that's where you guys end up."

"Wow," said Bear, turning to her, "that must be beauti-ful work." He had a way of bringing people in to him, of making them feel big and important, and he was a good lis-tener. I could see Nancy's eyes soften toward him; she liked talking about babies.

"It's the best job in the whole universe, far as I'm con-cerned," she said. "It makes me happy. Some days it's like I get to be a mother ten, twelve times. Yesterday we delivered four babies. Two sets of twins."

Luna came over from the sink, wiping her hands on a ragged towel. "I want to have the baby right here," she said, putting an arm around Bear's waist. "No offense, but I hate hospitals. Everyone I've ever lost died in a hospital bed."

Bear put an arm around her shoulder and pulled her into him tight, his face fixed on the wide floor planks.

"I understand," Nancy said. "You're right to do it here. Too many women are intimidated by birth. But it's what we were designed to do." She moved over to Luna and gently applied her hands to the other woman's belly. Luna moved Nancy's hands up, almost to her ribs.

"Feel that?" Luna asked.

"Little feet," said Nancy, beaming.

"Come here," Luna said. "I want to talk to you about my preparations." The two women went toward the kitchen area and I could see that Luna was pouring out two mugs of tea.

"How about those shots?" I said.

"Coming up," said Bear, and he poured an inch of whiskey in two juice glasses. We touched cups and drained them back quickly.

"Work!" he said loudly.

"Fatherhood!" I sang out.

And then we went out into the cold, where three old pickup trucks were already pulling off the country road and processing toward the church.

Bear and I always worked together each year, a team of two, taking turns with the chainsaws, tying off broken limbs with cable or chain, moving around the forest dissecting fallen trees and organizing the logs into stacks for other teams to take away, back to the splitters. It was a good day to be in the forest, the sun clear and warm despite the date, and we worked hard and silent until Bear wiped his brow and sat heavily on a wide ancient stump of a long-gone oak.

"I didn't want to be a father," he said. "Truth is, I'm scared shitless."

I shut the chainsaw off and for a moment we were engulfed in its blue smoke, the memory of its whine and roar still in our ears. I sat down beside him, and there was something inside me that hummed of satisfaction too, because in all things Bear's life had been his own without the slightest of concessions. He lived beautifully and effortlessly, and he was one of those people in life that people shake their heads at in wonder and envy. He was the kind of man who could get any woman at a party. Who could sit down at a piano and play so truthfully that his audience might quietly weep. Once I had seen him hit a baseball four hundred feet. The coach had stopped practice so that the team could measure his blast, all of us pacing off the distance past the outfield wall, the almost unfathomable numbers adding up in our heads. And then he quit baseball because he claimed it bored him.

"I think everyone must be," I said to him banally.

"I don't want it, though," he said. "That's the thing. I don't want it at all. She puts my hand on her stomach and I feel it move, but it just scares me. Like something is coming to get me."

I stayed quiet.

"She said it had to happen. That I hadn't married her right or something. That she'd had to sacrifice her life to live the way we do, and she said she deserved the baby and I owed it to her. She was talking about leaving," he said. "She convinced me that I would like it, but I know I won't because I don't want to. Maybe you could talk to her?"

I looked at him. "What am I supposed to say?"

"Never mind," he said, shaking his head. "No, look— Christ, you're right. I don't know what the hell is wrong with me."

We stayed that way a while, until the cold was in our sweaty garments, and then we stood slowly and went back to work, with much less vigor than when we had started. The sun looked silver in the sky, and overhead there was the sound of a crow flying through cold air, its wings like paper. Here and there throughout the woods I could see other pairs of workers laboring, their chainsaws buzzing, yellow dust going into the snow and air from the guts of the downed trees.

"I've never been trapped before," Bear said as he stacked pieces of cordwood, "not by anything. The other night her belly was against me in bed and I could feel the baby kicking my back. You imagine?"

"You'll be a great father," I lied.

He looked up at me then, squinting against the reflected sunlight on the snow, and he said, "I got a surprise for you."

He began moving off deeper into the forest and I followed him, as I always did, the chainsaw heavy in my hand, and

I watched as he moved quickly, with the ease and surefootedness of an animal, ducking low under branches or with long strides over fallen logs. We trudged past bur oaks and maples and aspens, through cedars and white pines, to the lip of the bluff where the world fell off into space, and below us was the blue line of a river whose name I did not know.

The tree was gargantuan, a behemoth cottonwood, and its roots seemed to hold the very cliff together, the subterranean fingers of the giant tree holding boulders in order like so many marbles. Bear began to climb the tree, leaving his chainsaw on the yellow rock below. I put my fingers in the gnarled bark of the tree and began working my way up too, racing him, in fact, the two of us winding separate paths up the tree, following different networks of branches into the heights, where a few dead leaves yet hung like strange laundry. We laughed out loud as we climbed, panting. The world beneath us white and forever unfurled. My lungs felt cold and huge.

"Nancy is beautiful," Bear said from his roost, though he was looking at the river below.

You have everything, I thought, nodding. "It'll be okay," I said to him, our comments like two planes passing in the heavens, miles apart.

"I don't think I'm meant to be with just one person," he said to me, and in his voice was a kind of mock sadness.

"Don't you love her?" I asked.

I had loved her many years ago, Shelly. But then, love was always my easiest emotion.

"Yes," he said slowly, then, "I don't know. I don't think I can share people. I want them to be all mine."

The sun was falling already, and the wind in the treetop made us shudder. I waited for Bear to begin his descent before doing the same. The climb down was terrifying, and I hung close to the cottonwood, unable to discern now the path I'd taken up the tree. Still midway up, I could see Bear already on the ground, chainsaw in his hand, already walking away.

"Bear!" I yelled.

He turned to me, "Get down already! Let's find some beer!"

My face was hot, windblown and sunburned despite the cold. "I can't!" I stammered.

He set the chainsaw down and came back to the trunk of the tree, "Move your left foot down into that little hollow there," he said with a patronizing kind of patience.

"I can't do it, Ben," I said, using the name he had abandoned long ago.

"Christ, man," he said, "I can't come up there and pull you down! I got to get back there and help Luna with dinner. You'll figure it out."

He picked up the chainsaw and moved off into the forest, leaving me up in the air, pressed against the rough trunk of the tree, whose limbs danced with the rising wind swirling up from the river bottom. The sun hovered over the western horizon and the bark of the tree was losing its warmth. I was thirty-odd feet off the ground.

———

Just before the fall of night, in the last of the gloaming, I slid down the tree in a fit of desperation, falling between branches in places, afraid of losing all my light and finding myself stranded over the cliff. I could hear the chainsaw party already kicking into gear as I moved through the forest, angry, cuts burning on my face and hands from the climb down. The chainsaw felt oddly light in my hands as I approached the light of the bonfire and the sound of thick lubricious laughter.

A small group of men were blowing gasoline out of their mouths into the fire, and the flames were booming up into the soft new night, sparks breaking up into the black and blue evening. A bearded man was sawing against his fiddle, and the music sounded like something carnal and antique. In the shadows I saw the pit where the pig had been roasted, its carcass now a mess of flesh laid bare and people were picking at the rags of meat with their fingers, their faces greasy with work and hunger. I went to the barrel of beer, which sat heavily in a snowbank like a very fat man, and I drank from the spigot until I felt warm with something other than anger. I wanted very badly to leave the chainsaw party, but I could see that my truck was blocked in by other vehicles, and besides, I could not leave without Nancy, wherever she was. I began searching the shadowy faces of the party. In the air hung thick tendrils of marijuana smoke, and I could see that two women were lying in the snow, forming the imprints of angels with their outstretched legs and arms.

It was Luna that found me, wandering the woods, after I interrupted two lovers moving against the night: a woman bent over a pile of firewood and her lover entering her from behind, their asses glowing in the darkness. I had come upon them quietly, not even comprehending at first, and then afraid that it might be Nancy, and at last the man had turned to me and said, "You want a turn?" his dick in his hand like a skeleton key. Then the woman grabbed his narrow hips and moved him back into her, laughing.

I had turned away and begun wandering away from the lights, mumbling Nancy's name, when Luna grabbed my shoulder with one hand, a lantern glowing in the other and swinging, its golden light illuminating the detritus of the forest floor.

"Noah!" she shouted. "Noah!"

I fell down in the snow and sat that way, looking up at her, this woman I had known when we were two fumbling teenagers, kids really, necking on a mattress in the bed of my pickup truck as a drive-in movie lit the summer nights and I remembered the fireflies I sometimes found in her red hair, the paleness of her white skin. "Shelly," I said. "Shelly, I feel drunk."

She kneeled in the snow and touched my face with her gloved hands.

"Christ, your face is a mess," she said, laughing softly, her fingers under my chin. Her eyes were wet.

"I'm so happy for you," I said. "You'll make a great mother." I was not lying, and the thought of her holding a baby made me want to weep with happiness and longing and then I did begin to cry, the tears on my face hot and painful on the new cuts and scrapes covering my face.

Since the moment I met Nancy I had wanted very badly to be a father, a dad. It was the night of Thanksgiving Day. I had taken my mother into the hospital. She had cut her hand while carving the turkey. I remember her standing at the sink, running the tap over her bleeding fingers, all the color draining from her face. "It'll be okay," she said to me, quickly covering the wound with a towel. "No way, Mom," I said, and we drove to the ER, where we sat for ten minutes in a waiting room watching highlights of the morning's parade in a faraway city. They took her into the ER and I sat leafing through some battered magazines.

After some length of time, I stood up and began wandering the hospital. I found the neonatal wing, the nursery, with its rows of babies lying in small transparent bins, not cribs, but trays, all of their little heads covered in blue or pink hats, bodies tightly swaddled. Some slept and some cried out. Nancy moved from baby to baby, picking them up and holding them to her chest. She swayed with them in her arms, like slow dancing, her lips close to their little heads. I watched her, transfixed, until my own mother was standing beside me, her finger bandaged. She pressed against me warmly and I was not embarrassed. Nancy had not noticed us.

"You were such a beautiful baby," my mother said. "We loved you even before you were born."

I didn't say anything, my eyes still on Nancy, my body suddenly loose and relaxed amid the ambient sounds of the hospital everywhere, the relative cool and dimness of the building. The beautiful woman swaying before me, behind a giant pane of glass separating us from all those very small faces. I found myself happily drowsy.

"You'll have your chance," my mother said.

But I already had the sense even before seeing a doctor about it that I would never conceive a child, that something was broken inside me. There were moments in my life that I might have pointed to by way of explanation—the serrated tip of a figure skate, the cleated foot of a runaway fullback, moments when my anatomy had suffered specific insults. But the more I yearned for fatherhood, the more I understood somehow that any child I might raise into an adult would not be the product of my genetic line. I would be some kind of surrogate. And so, accepting that deficiency within me, I had begun waiting for orphans to enter my life, like figures of golden light.

I came back to the hospital one day later, a bouquet of flowers in my hands, and found Nancy. Her coworkers blushed and then applauded quietly, their eyes dancing uncertainly. I had just gotten my hair cut and even gone to the local men's clothing store, where I bought a navy blue suit coat with shiny brass buttons. She was holding a baby, of course. A new girl named Daphne.

Shelly breathed in deeply. "I want to leave this place. Will you take me?" she asked.

"Why?" I asked.

She erased the wetness of my face with her fingers.

"Let's go," she said, lifting me up.

"I have to get Nancy," I insisted.

"Don't. Don't go looking."

"But I have to. She came with me. I love her."

The bonfire was out of control, and as we skirted the edge of the party, there was a man juggling three chainsaws in the air, all of the machines rasping and grumbling, and each time one of the chainsaws fell into his hands, he revved up its small engine and the teeth of the saw went round and round, sharp and shining in the grimy light. The violinist was sweating profusely even though he wore no shirt, and the bow he used to make the music that went out into the night moved furiously against the cold strings of the instrument. There was nothing left of the pig when we walked by the pit, just the face of a misbegotten animal and its four still hooves.

Inside the church candles were swaying on the window-sills and many bodies were laid out over the floor. A man was walking between the figures, and in his hands were doses of acid. The supplicants extended their tongues as if in acceptance of a communion wafer. They were listening to an opera screech out of the ornate horn of a hand-cranked Victrola, powered by a man in the darkness, working its crank as needed.

I found them in the loft. Nancy on a bed, sitting on his face, his beard billowed out around her crotch. That was the last time I ever saw her, her hands holding her own head and hair and his fingers in her mouth, her breasts heavy and beautiful inside the church, where the light of the bonfire seeped in through the tall stained-glass windows and made the building a kind of terrible hallucination I will never forget.

Shelly was outside the church, a bag in her hand.

"I could burn the place down," she said.

"Let's go," I said, taking her bag and throwing it into the bed of my truck.

"You're parked in," Shelly said.

"Wait beside the road," I said.

She went off into the darkness and I climbed into the truck and revved the engine. I yanked the transmission into reverse and stepped down hard on the gas pedal. The big black pipes of the truck went back into the car behind me and pushed it several feet into the next vehicle. There was the sound of breaking glass and broken metal. Then I dropped the truck into drive and plowed forward, slamming the vehicle in front of me ten feet ahead and sending it toward the bonfire, where the music suddenly stopped, all three flying chainsaws landing in the snow. I put the truck in reverse once more, demolishing another vehicle before finally pulling out onto the road and waiting for Shelly. She moved into the truck gingerly, holding her belly, and then I slid the truck into gear and we left the derelict church and all those beaten automobiles and the bonfire and the pig and the secret new lovers and a disembodied Italian soprano, wailing into the night.

I raised Samuel with love and fervor, and though he grew up into a boy who appeared in so many ways as his father had in my own childhood, I was comforted at times by his deep blue eyes and dark hair. When Samuel and I went fishing or traipsing through the forest in search of morels or fiddleheads, and I might glance his way, there were times in which I found myself time traveling, back into a past when Bear and I were tightly bonded friends exploring the world together.

Many years after that chainsaw party I attended, we drove by the church on a cold, bright winter solstice afternoon. It was just a lark, a drive through the countryside, with enough time and psychic distance that neither of us cared, I suppose, if we saw Bear or Nancy off in the distance, perhaps pulling their own children on a sled through the December snow. Shelly had said, "I'd like to have a look, one more time." So the three of us piled into the pickup truck and drove that way, southwest toward the great river. But there was no soirée. The woods all around the church were utterly free of any chainsaw cacophony, and when we passed the church it looked abandoned, a great plank nailed to the two front doors. The white paint of the steeple and chapel were chipping badly and a few of the window-panes had been broken and were spider-webbed with cracks.

"I wonder where they are," I said.

"Who?" asked Samuel.

"Some old friends," said Shelly, though there was no soft-ness to her voice.

"Your mom used to live here," I said.

Samuel quickly turned his head and stared at Shelly. "That place?" he asked.

"You were almost born in that church," she said.

"I'm glad I wasn't," he said, fidgeting on the seat. "It looks haunted."

Then we drove off, away from the church and the site of all those chainsaw parties, and many years later I would learn that the volunteer fire department had burnt it down to the blackened earth. I had run into one of the volunteer firemen at a wedding, and he described the church in de-tail to me, saying, "After we lit the fire, it went up quickly, and then you wouldn't believe it, from underneath the place hundreds of snakes came out and half the department ran off. I never seen anything like it."

"They used to have parties at that church," I said, "chain-saw parties. That's how I met my wife."

RAINWATER

THE OLD MAN and his grandson sat on the porch swing watching it rain. They swung according to the old man's rhythm; the little boy's feet dangling, his shoelaces untied, still inches off the sinking porch. Water collected in the grooves of the dirt and grass two-track driveway, and toward the barn chickens bobbed their heads and cooed low, high-stepping as they pulled earthworms free from the saturated black soil. A flag drooped heavy on its rusted and listing pole.

"Where's my mom?" the boy asked, not unhappily. He wiped his nose and looked at the old man, who simply stared off, away, blinking his pale blue eyes slowly. "Grandpa?"

The old man scooted his grandson closer, rubbed his towhead with a thick old hand. She was late, a day late, and every number the old man dialed went unanswered. He could not say that she was in danger; she was wild and always had been. She dropped the boy with him on Friday afternoons, like a package. Left him without food or toys and sometimes without extra clothing. What did the old man know about taking care of a child?

So Friday nights he and the boy drove into town, ate supper at the diner beside the railroad tracks, watched passing trains, shared a sundae. Drove to the hardware store and bought die-cast trucks and tractors, little-boy underwear, overalls, thick socks, T-shirts, and sweat shirts. The little boy falling asleep across the bench seat of the old man's pickup truck as they jostled down county roads and toward the fallow farm, where the old man would park, admiring this little boy before lifting him out and carrying him inside, to his own bed, where he lay the boy and pulled the sheets and the gray wool blanket up and over his shoulders and kissed his forehead and touched his little-boy ears and then sat listening to his alarm clock tick and waiting for the sound of his daughter's car to come down the driveway until at last he went to the kitchen and poured himself a cup of cold coffee and wrung his hands and wondered silently how he had failed her.

"Hold on a minute," the old man said. "Hold still. Be back in a minute."

"Grandpa," the boy said tentatively, and the old man recognized the edge of fear in the boy's voice, at the thought of being abandoned for even a second. The boy looked at him balefully.

The old man motioned through the screen door, inside the house. He cleared his throat. "I've got to pee."

The little boy nodded uncertainly, and the old man went inside, careful not to let the screen door slam. Walked through the sitting room with its ancient TV and grandfather clock and duck paintings and dusty duck decoys and taxidermied deer mounts and tired furniture. Into the bathroom he went, closing the door lightly, and wiped beads of sweat from his forehead. Maybe, he thought, she wasn't coming home this time. His urine came haltingly. He stood in front of the mirror afterward and washed his hands, looked at his face: his white hair, the broken blood vessels across his nose and cheekbones, the loose skin beneath his chin like that of a turkey, two days' worth of whiskers. I ought to look better for him, he thought. I have to be strong.

From the porch he heard a little voice: "*Grandpa, Grandpa, Grandpa* . . ."

In the kitchen he found a tin cup, then padded back to the boy on the swing, who sat smiling up at him.

"Here," the old man said, handing the boy the cup.

The boy looked down into the cup. "It's empty."

"You ever drink rain?"

"No, Mom won't let me go out in the rain."

"Well, I'm saying that you can."

"It's okay. I'm not that thirsty."

"Well, all right then, go get me a cup."

The boy slid off the swing, approached the edge of the porch, where the stairs descended into overgrown grass and dandelions. He held the cup out. Rain fell off the eaves in big slow measured drops. The old man moved to the swing, watching, with arms crossed. Parenting, he remembered, was all about creating work, jobs, games.

"No, go on out there," he said. "Go out in the rain now. Get me some fresh stuff. I don't want that runoff from the roof. Go on now. Don't worry 'bout getting wet."

The boy stepped into the rain, droplets turning the blue cotton of his shirt a color closer to black. The rain began to slick back his hair; he laughed. "It's warm."

The old man smiled behind a hand. "Go on. Get me some of that fresh rain."

The boy moved farther away from the porch, a thick shoal of gray clouds slung low overhead. He held the cup out away from him, then over his head.

"Grandpa? What does rain taste like?" the boy called out.

"Clouds, I suppose. Mostly like clouds."

The boy brought the cup down, glanced inside the little vessel. "Is this enough?"

"Sure, sure it is. Bring it up here. You won't drink, I sure will."

The boy scrambled up the steps onto the porch, careful not to spill. He passed the cup cleanly to his grandfather, jumped onto the swing, and sat, hands in his lap, looking at his grandfather.

The old man held the cup in his hands for some time, looking at the water there. I don't know that I have ever tasted rain, he thought. He tried to recall some summer afternoon, some spring evening, when, perhaps out walking with his wife in town or on the tractor, or even back in his war time, when he might have opened his mouth for a raindrop to find or held his helmet out like a cup, when his young tongue might have slipped out of his mouth to lick rain-slicked lips. But nothing came to him.

"Grandpa?"

"You take the first sip. Go on. You collected it, you ought to drink it."

"Really?"

"Sure. It's yours."

The boy raised the cup to his lips and took a small noisy sip. The old man watched him.

"Well?"

"Good. It tastes good, I guess. You want some, Grandpa?"

"Sure, sure I do. Here, hand that thing here."

They sat that way, the old man swinging them, his right hand on one of the chains that kept the swing moored to the ceiling of the porch. Now the air smelled of ozone and the rain came harder, more violently. The ground trembled with faraway lightning and there was the guttural sound of thunder. The boy inched closer to his grandfather, collapsing what little distance there remained. The old man placed his hand on the boy's head, the air charged with electricity and their skin almost wet, the hairs on their arms at attention, like two scared cats.

The old man raised the cup to his mouth and sipped. A lightning bolt, blue and hot white, split the sky not a mile away, and the thunder that filled their ears not even a second later seemed impossibly big, made them jump. The air sizzled. The old man imagined his daughter. Was she driving toward them, her windshield wipers frantically casting water toward the yellow center line? Or was she blissed out somewhere, a belt cinched around her pale, skinny arm, eyes half shut, slumped halfway out of a chair and resting on a dirty floor? Or in a motel room with two strangers, sipping her favorite, Southern Comfort, out of clear plastic cups and the tapping and scraping of credit cards making fine white lines on the bedside table? Or someplace much worse: a shallow ditch, a dank basement, the hot dark trunk of a sedan, a Greyhound bus, a hospital—where, where, where?

He drank the remainder of the rainwater and began rocking them with more vigor. He hugged the child fiercely, felt his own lips meeting the top of the boy's head.

"Come on," he said, "let's go inside. Get you a hot shower and those clothes in the dryer."

"Grandpa," the boy said, "could you taste the clouds?"

The old man looked toward the flooded driveway, held the cup in his hands, so small.

"Grandpa?"

"Come on," the old man said. "I'm not gonna ask you twice."

Inside, the old man drew a hot bath, steam warming the small white-tiled bathroom. Behind him, the little boy removed his clothing, then stood on tiptoe and peed into the toilet. When the old man stood and shook his red hand of the hot bathwater, there was his grandson, stark naked, pale and smiling. The old man handed him a new bar of soap.

"When you're done, call me, and I'll bring a warm towel." The old man averted his eyes. So long since he'd seen another person naked, least of all a child. "I'm gonna throw these clothes in the dryer."

In the basement, he tossed the ball of wet clothing into the dryer and started the machine. The whitewashed walls of the cellar bled with rainwater, and in the dark corners of the damp room, an unseen cricket sounded slowly. He sighed deeply. More thunder, even closer this time. The single hanging lightbulb flickered. The floorboards above him seemed to shiver. He took the stairs slowly. He could hear the water still running in the bathtub, the little boy talking, *singing* to himself.

The old man walked out to the porch, held his bony shoulders in his hands. He kicked peeling paint off the floorboards with his boots; great chips sloughed off and then went sailing out into the yard. Sat down heavily in the swing, watched his driveway become an ephemeral stream, and waited for his grandson to say his name.

SVEN & LILY

SVEN WAS SEVEN FEET TALL. He was a beanpole of a guy with a little paunch of a belly and big goofy hair that he was always combing. At bars he stood behind the scrum at the rail and looked at his hair in the mirror behind the bottles and coiffed that kahuna wave of a thing up another four inches on his head. Sven and my wife went to med school, and she was always trying to get us together. To make us buddies, like you do with little kids or maybe dogs, I don't know. You push two things close enough that they become one thing.

Sven was good people, and I didn't know at first if we could be friends. He was smart. Smarter than me by a country mile. He read biographies of the presidents for fun, and had opinions about the Episcopal church and fuel efficiency and even good Southern barbecue. He didn't give you that vibration of a guy who liked to drink or smoke or steal looks at women, either. And he was tall. Sven was close to a foot and a half taller than me. He called me Lily, for Lilliputian. Nobody had ever given me a nickname before Sven; even my wife didn't call me honey or sugar. But when we were at the bar, shooting stick or throwing darts, he wouldn't call me Lily because he didn't want other people to get the idea that *he* thought I was small or deserved a girl's name or whatever. But I started to think of myself as Lily, and if you asked me what my name was at a bar, a few beers into things, I might tell you it was Lily.

We became partners, Sven and I. We looked after each other. Like brothers, but closer too, because most brothers I know aren't half as close as me and Sven were. Sven would go to the wood for you. He was loyal, dependable, I'll say that. The kind of guy you can count on, which seems to me to be a diminishing resource these days. He didn't have much meat on his bones, but he was rangy and he could grab dudes before they got to him. Once he had them, I'd come along with a pool cue or an eight ball and do the rest. But Sven was good people always. He didn't start those things, and I don't mean that we were always mixing things up, because we weren't.

But we would a little.

Sven didn't like to fight. Bad guys found him because he was a giant, and bad guys always want to take a swing at the giant. In the end, we almost always made friends with the bad guys too, Sven throwing his long arms around them like lassos, bringing them in, making them smile.

"See," he'd say, "that was stupid. Stupid fun. You gotta get me to the floor! You don't fight a tower by climbing up its side. You knock the goddamn tower down with a stick of dynamite! But I tell you this, Spider, I like you! I like your spirit!"

Sven was good with names. When he met people, he squinted down at their faces while he was pumping their hands, and in this way he took a mental Polaroid of them. He walked into bars and befriended everyone, learned their names and the names of their partners. He could win over anyone. One minute a guy was swinging at Sven's chin with a glass beer mug; the next, Sven had him in a headlock, rubbing his bony fists into the guy's scalp, asking, "What's your name? Huh? What's your name? Not gonna' stop 'til I get a name!"

Finally the guy would break, worn down and embarrassed. "Fuck it! Spider! Okay, goddamnit, I'm Spider!"

"Well, all right, Spider," Sven would say. "I think you owe me and my buddy here a drink."

And so Spider or whoever would buy, and after we'd left the bar that night, we'd all be peeing in the alley together, or maybe weaving our way to the nearest KFC to split a bucket of chicken. And Sven would've added him to our ad hoc army of barroom confederates.

Sven was like that. Before med school, he was an engineer. Wicked smart. He could build you a bridge or a goddamn motor and the next minute give you sound advice on your taxes or an invention idea that your dad had scrawled out on a napkin. His mind worked in mathematics and angles. He told me that he liked having me around because I had a low center of gravity. He said I was his pit bull Lily, and thereafter that's just how I thought of myself, as a pit bull, or maybe like the pit bull was my spirit animal. Like an emblem or a logo that is more what you are than what you are really. I even started carrying myself like a dog, my shoulders all balled up around my head. At night I did push-ups and crunches until my gut disappeared and what was left over became all bulging ab muscles. I began looking like a linebacker.

Sven was one of those guys your wife puts you with because she sees only the good in him, and she thinks that maybe if you just buddy up with him, you'll get better too. My wife saw white light coming out of Sven's eyes and asshole. To her, he farted choral music or those big damp notes of the organ at church.

Kids loved Sven. They loved his cartoon name, his cartoon hair, his cartoon giant size. They swung off his ropy arms like playground equipment. They shrieked with laughter at the size of his hands. Slid their miniature feet into the dark caverns of his shoes and giggled themselves wet plodding around our house, or Sven and Tessa's apartment.

My daughter loved Sven, which was only further evidence for my wife that Sven was magical.

"Mr. Sven?" Lola asked one night when he was over.

"Yes, Peanut," he said.

"Do you like Girl Scout Cookies?"

"I love Girl Scout Cookies."

"Would you buy some of my Girl Scout Cookies?"

"Of course. Do you have Oreos?"

"No!" Lola laughed.

"Do you have . . . Nilla Wafers?"

"No!"

"Do you have . . . Thin Mints?"

"Yes!"

"Okay. I'll take five boxes of Thin Mints."

Lola clapped her hands and leapt off the ground. Then she became shy again. Folded her hands. Looked from Sven to the ground.

"How tall are you, Mr. Sven?" she giggled.

"Thirty feet tall," he answered, straight-faced and nonchalant.

"No!" she cried. "How tall are you *really*, Mr. Sven? How tall?"

"Ah, let me think," Sven said, nursing a bottle of beer. "Fifteen feet tall."

Whereupon Lola's mouth went slack, into a kind of incredible O. She walked over to my wife, Nadine, and whispered into her ear, "Mr. Sven is fifteen feet tall. And he's going to buy five boxes of my cookies!"

"He is a very tall man," my wife said, winking at Sven as I cleared empty beer and wine bottles and swept Lola's crumbs into my empty hands.

———

Sven liked pool. Maybe because his height meant that no shot on the green table was an impossibility. His long fingers made perfect bridges. His engineering mind found the truest angles and shortcuts and banks. His medical mind pieced out the logic and practicality of his most geometric shots. His only handicap was the pool-hall lamps that hung low over the verdant tables. Sometimes I would hold the lamp off to the side for him as he stretched out over the table like a praying mantis.

"Stupid lights," he would say, motioning to the odd scars on his forehead, courtesy of various collisions with hanging things.

We became friends, real friends, shooting stick. Two grown men orbiting the green felt of the table. Organizing the rainbow of balls. Spinning the cue under a blue cube of chalk. Orchestrating the jukebox. Wilson Pickett. Sam & Dave. Gladys Knight & the Pips. The Rolling Stones. Sven and I never walked into a bar or pool hall without a soundtrack in mind. And I liked Sven because he had a sense of fairness that is rare in most watering holes. We took turns buying each other beers, gave each other quarters or dollar bills for the Wurlitzer. When our guts were full of beer and we had to return to our wives, we'd sit down together to eat, alternating as to who grabbed the check. Sven took care of me, and I tried to take care of him too.

I knew that with me, he could be someone different. Not just the future doctor who'd been an engineer. He could be a little bad too. Or at least he could *play* bad, mix it up a little, rub up against a skirt in a bar and not worry that the news was going to get back to his wife. If he got scraped up in a fight I'd tell Tessa that he'd had one too many beers and gouged his head into a billiards lamp hung too low over the table. That sort of thing.

"If he wasn't so tall," she'd say, shaking her head and putting her arms around his narrow waist. Sven was her baby. Her great big too-tall, skinny baby. Sometimes at the end of an evening, I'd hear her talking to him, whispering into his ear, almost the way you might talk to a baby, all molasses and maple syrup poetry. Her fingernails were long, with deep burgundy polish, and she liked to stroke his long goofy face with those nails. But I liked Tessa very much. Sven deserved a woman like her.

Sven liked me, I think, because I knew where the trouble was and how to get close to it without getting burned or scarred too much. Sven and my wife were older than the other med school students, who were mostly just kids, still fighting back greasy faces smudged in acne. Still rubbing up against one another in too-expensive bars, trading diseases like baseball cards. Sven and Tessa came over to our place almost once a week for dinner or brunch, but Sven and I hung out once a week for sure.

"You and Sven," said my wife, "you guys sure hang out a lot. Should I be jealous?"

"Nah," I'd say. "Poor guy just needs to blow off some steam."

"Sven?" she'd say. "There's no steam in Sven. He's mellow yellow."

"I don't know about that," I'd say. "I've seen him get wild a few times." I never talked about the fights, the alleyway pukes, the occasional bathroom joint.

"I don't believe it," she'd say seriously. "Engineers don't even have that in them."

"Yeah, but he's going to be a doctor," I'd argue. "Doctors have egos. Doctors need to let their steam out too. All that stress you guys are under?"

"Not Sven," she'd say. "He's too sweet."

It irked me, to tell you the truth, her inability to see him the way I was able to. It made me feel jealous, I guess, as if I was worth less than he was. It made me feel heavy with knowledge too, and if it hadn't been Sven, I swear I would have blown her vision of him into a million little pieces. But when you know someone like Sven, you defend him, because you want there to be good people in the world and it doesn't do anyone any good to break them down into something as bad and ugly as everyone else.

"Yeah," I said. "You're probably right."

———

One night I picked Sven up in our beater Toyota Camry. It took him a long time to fold himself into that little car, even with the passenger seat pushed as far back as it could go. He rode around town with his knees near his chest, hugging them through his pants. He rolled the window down, and I watched as he lapped up the first warm spring air, like a happy golden retriever, cheeks and lips practically flapping in the wind, gums bright pink, his too-large teeth immaculately white. I rubbed my tongue over my own teeth, stained yellow brown from too much coffee and a chewing tobacco habit that I kept secret from everyone but Sven. I offered him the pouch of shredded tobacco. He loved to chew tobacco with me and had begun bringing a toothbrush with him when we went out so that he could brush his teeth before I returned him home to Tessa.

He pinched a generous helping of the tobacco from the pouch and tucked it into his mouth for his molars to grind, then smiled like a chipmunk, and we both spat out our windows, careful not to streak the car with brown, tobacco-flecked juice. Evidence of our shenanigans.

"Goddamn!" said Sven, tapping out a rhythm on the roof of the Japanese automobile. "Where we going tonight? Shoot some stick? Toss some darts? What're you up for, Lily? Huh? What's the plan, Lily-man!"

I did have the evening mapped out, actually, into a kind of plan. I had heard of a bar out in the country, a half hour's drive, with a pool table Minnesota Fats had once played on and whose name was supposedly etched in the side of the table like a goddamn testament from God.

Sven seemed tickled. "I want to touch his name," he said, with some gravity. "I want to run that table like it was a basement floor. I want those balls dropping into rabbit holes."

He spat out into the countryside, already all around us, the sky loud with the wings of Canada geese, the world thick with the perfume of freshly spread cowshit. It made me happy to see Sven already so carefree, even before the beer or the billiards. Before we even stepped into yet another dark, dense rectangular bunker of a building and began punching numbers and letters on a new jukebox. We were a missile in that little car, a billiards-seeking missile with two passengers on a guided course toward a happy motherfucking target.

The bar was at a crossroads of country lanes and soybean fields with a gravel parking lot and an abundance of neon glowing in the windows like some pirate casino shipwrecked out on the lonely prairie. We left the Toyota in the lot, among all the Fords and Chevrolets, where it looked utterly out of place. We spat out our tobacco, our heads fuzzy, warm, and reeling.

Sven entered the bar first, ducking under the low doorway, me following behind him like an early-afternoon shadow smaller than its maker. We found stools at the bar and ordered a couple of tappers as we took in the place and found the table, on one end of the bar under a cone of yellow light, its felt not the dense Technicolor green of a new table but a pale, well-used green ripped and patched in places, its rails hard and fast and brutalized. It was a crabgrass gravel sand-lot of a pool table.

"Fast table," said Sven.

"She's seen better days," I said. "I'm gonna pump the juke."

It was a hillbilly/yokel jukebox chock-full of dated singles, almost like a time capsule intended to teach the history of country and western music. I played the standards: Hank Senior, Patsy Cline, Merle Haggard, Bob Wills, and then some "newish" stuff to placate the younger regulars: Clint Black, George Strait, and Garth, but steering clear of the teenybopper BS.

Sven had already moved over to the table. The balls were big confetti on the abused felt, and he raked them in the triangle. Then he began moving around the table, touching all the surfaces with his hands, like they do in movies when someone is looking for the entrance to a secret passage. I watched him from the juke, my tapper already mostly gone.

I watched as he stood up quickly and said, "Found it! I found him!"

"Sweet!" I ordered another and walked over to the table.

The man's name was carved near the quarters slot. Four letters, carved deep and crude into the wood: FATS. I touched his name and voltage went through me, electrified my finest hairs, curled my toes. I had touched Jim Morrison's tombstone once, on a family vacation to France. It was like that. Like what I imagined God and Adam touching fingers felt in that painting on the ceiling of the Sistine Chapel. Electricity.

"I'll be," Sven murmured approvingly, scratching at the scant whiskers peppering his checks. "How many pool tables in the world can brag that Minnesota Fats broke their balls? Huh? Not too many, I'd say."

We shook our heads in wonder and took a few long sips off our beers. Then Sven pointed to me and I selected a cue off the wall and broke.

Sometimes a bar is like a cocoon or a womb, a place you wish you never had to leave. Everything you need is there: cold beer, familiar music, frozen pizza thin as paper, warm cashews if you're lucky. Baseball or football on the television. Jerky in a jar. Pickled pig's feet. If you're good people, if you're punching the juke and minding your business, people take care of you too, in a way that doesn't really happen in the real world. The house buys you a drink, maybe. The bartender says she likes your taste in music and slips you a fiver to keep the machine humming.

I had gone to the bar to order some more beers, leaving Sven at the table, where he was racking. He liked to rack, insisted that a broken triangle of balls was like a bad foundation; the rest of the game was then broken too, and suspect. He was good at racking, and I'd seen him rerack a set of balls five, six, seven times, laboring to unify them *just so*. Rolling them around the table again and again and snapping them into rigid formation.

"Two more," I told the bartender, an older woman with a hard-worn face, an unlit cigarette dangling loose between chapped lips.

"Looks like your buddy has a friend," she said, nodding toward the table.

I'd looked away for only a second, but there was a beautiful blonde moving toward Sven in a languid kind of sashay, jeans tight on long, long legs; it was excruciatingly wonderful watching her move. Her waist was impossibly narrow, and even from my vantage across the room at the bar, I could make out a set of high cheekbones and bee-stung lips that reminded me of a Russian ballerina.

"Where the hell'd *she* come from?" I said to myself, drinking fast and trying to piece together the world in front of me.

"Careful with that one, though," said the bartender. "She's a goddamn man assassin. Eats 'em alive. Her there, she's been divorced thrice."

I held up three fingers, brows raised. The bartender nodded gravely.

"She looks a little young for that," I offered lamely.

"They start early 'round here. Anyway, you watch out for your friend."

"Oh, Sven'll be okay."

She was near the cues, touching them, and she selected

one from the forest of other sticks and motioned to the table. I could see a shit-eating grin crack over Sven's face like he'd won at bingo or found a twenty-dollar bill on the sidewalk.

Maybe I should and maybe I shouldn't have, but I left the bar just then for a dip of tobacco and a sip of my beer. A girl like that was something out of a dream or a movie, and I didn't want to watch Sven or be around for whatever happened. There was something almost pornographic about the scene that I didn't want to be an audience member of, although that hadn't stopped the rest of the bar, rubbernecking for all they were worth. No, I'd seen enough, thank you. Sven was laboring toward a secret I didn't need to be privy to the details of. I couldn't lie to Nadine about a crime I didn't witness.

Outside the bar, the stars were out, all of them. A billion profusions of light, and closer in, a matrix of lightning bugs hovering off the earth, their own galaxy, blinking on and off and flying their loopy green circuits. I watched the progress of a satellite and spat into the parking lot, feeling my body go limp, the edges of the planet soft and fuzzy. It felt like maybe I was about to drift off into my own orbit, out over the soybeans and corn, over the silos and barns, and I have to say, I was ready for that strange levitation. Ready to start my ascent to wherever, ready to feel weightless, the cord linking me to my known life snipped sharp and clean. And I wanted that lift-off too, just to float off away from everything for a while, only to come back, slide back between my own bedsheets beside Nadine, her naked shoulder alpine and creamy smooth above the sheets.

Just then Sven burst out of the bar, the skinny girl behind him, her lipstick a little smeared and the top button of her jeans loudly unbuttoned. It broke me from my spell.

"Go, go, gogoogogo!" Sven said, pushing me with his hands, shooing me toward the Camry. I fumbled for the keys, dropped them in the dust and gravel of the lot and got to my knees, looking to find them.

"God damn it, I'm drunk," I slurred.

Sven scooped the keys off the earth in a kind of motion I have seen performed only in jai alai videos and dragged me up too, up off the parking lot, throwing me into the car and somehow bending underneath the wheel and gunning the small engine within a matter of seconds. Sitting in the passenger seat, more than a little stunned, I realized that I had swallowed my chew of Red Man. I would pay for that later, I knew.

"What's the fucking problem?" I said. "Was she *too* beautiful? Jesus! I thought we were having a nice time!" I watched her figure shrink in the side mirror and even gave her a sad little wave.

But Sven was vigorously shaking his head and touching his neck with those long fingers. He looked like a man bitten by a she-vampire.

"You all right?" I asked, coming up out of it, trying to clear my head.

"You left me!" he said. "You left me, Lily!" He punched

the steering wheel and the horn beeped feebly in the night. He punched it again and we flew through the humidity of the evening like some drunk bird, squawking obnoxiously as the countryside tore past.

"Jesus, Sven, I'm sorry, I thought you were cool. I mean, she was beautiful."

"I can't fuck up," he said. "*All right?* I can't fuck up."

"What are you talking about?" I asked, confused.

"I can't do that, man. I just can't do that kind of shit." He was almost chanting it, as much to himself as to me.

"She gave me a hickey," he said, motioning sternly to his throat, where the bruise seemed to glow boldly, one link in an otherwise invisible necklace.

I started laughing, then caught myself, choking on it. Sven punched me good in the arm.

"What the fuck am I supposed to tell Tessa!" he said. "Huh? What the fuck!"

He hit the brakes just then, pulling over too quickly, and my head went into the dashboard. Hard. I knew my nose was broken from the blood in my mouth and down my throat, the iron taste of cutlery there, like sucking on a butter knife.

"Aw, Christ," Sven said. "Fuck, I should have warned you. I just . . . I don't know what the hell is happening to me tonight. I'm sorry, man. I'm so sorry about all this."

He reached over with his long arms and hugged me. We were two men in the countryside, embracing each other. One bleeding badly, the other with a neck sucked raw by a

Russian ballerina succubus. The world was quiet and densely humid. There were frogs in the ditches, croaking and groaning. The brake lights of the Camry glowed red against the night behind us and I was happy for the gentle glare. Even though I loved Sven, I did not want to die in that way, rear-ended by some farmer with a sixer on the bench seat of his pickup.

"What am I going to tell Tessa?" he asked me, his body draped over me, sniffles of fear and regret coming from his mouth and nose.

"All right, all right," I said. "Get off me for a second so I can stop this bleeding."

I reached into the backseat and grabbed some Kleenex to stuff my nose.

We sat in the car halfway off the road and ruminated. I hadn't realized how drunk Sven was, and now I knew, as I snuck a glance at him behind the wheel, his eyes filled with tears, his long fingers again on his neck, his pompadour totally askew. I didn't want him getting in trouble, either, and I knew that I wasn't going to come out on top of this one, unscathed or unpunished.

"All right," I said. "I got it. Get out of the car."

And that was how we came to fight each other in the middle of county highway DD, in the red lights of my Camry. It wasn't much of a fight, because it didn't need to be. I instructed Sven to bend down a bit so that I didn't have to jump when I punched him, and I had him close his eyes. I slugged him under the right eye, closer to the cheekbone, and he went down on the asphalt, laughing and then feeling the pain like a scrape against cement.

"Now," I said, "I'm sorry, but we need to add some more love bruises to that giraffe neck of yours."

I've never seen a man so happy to take a punch as Sven was then, and after a few more hooks and uppercuts we took a break, panting on the asphalt, my knuckles bloody on their stumps, my hands tired and sore. I stood up underneath the bath of starlight. Sven did too. I took a deep breath.

"Now me," I said. "Just not the teeth, okay?" A moment later I frowned, eyeing his incoming fist. It reminded me of Little League. The many times I stood terrified in the batter's box, waiting to be nailed by a pitch that only ever landed in the catcher's mitt.

But this time, I was well beaned.

We pulled up in front of their apartment and Sven shook my hand. He looked at me seriously and happily, and I could see that the fight or the rest of the drive had sobered him up.

"Got your story straight?" I asked.

"Do you?" he asked.

"A bad fight in a redneck bar. We tried to break it up, and instead the bar turned against us. We were so drunk we probably couldn't find the place with a map."

"That's a big ten-four," he said, and we shook hands again.

"Bullshit!" said Nadine. "Bullshit! Bullshit! Bullshit! I don't believe that crock for a second. Couldn't find the bar with a map. Tried to break up a fight! You know that after you passed out last night Tessa calls me at three o clock in the morning. Says Sven has a black eye and a cut lip. Says there is blood all over his clothes. Bruises all over his neck! What the hell?"

I decided to really sell that neck part. I could see that even if she didn't believe all the details, the lie was doing its work. We had juked them, deked them off their skates. The Russian ballerina was lost on that limitless prairie of lightning bugs and dive bars, and Nadine and Tessa were never going to be the wiser.

"Whaddaya want me to say?" I said feebly, apologetically, "One of those redneck bastards had a sleeper hold on Sven, and I really thought we'd had it. Lights out, you know? But then I got a boot to that guy's toes and Sven was able to break loose. Tell you what, wouldn't want to see what that guy looks like today. No, sir."

I sucked air through my nostrils, still throbbing with pain. It was a Wednesday morning before Nadine had to leave for school with Lola, and I had already called in sick to work, thinking that if I could fake illness the next two days I might be healed up for next week and never have to explain myself to the boss. I took a long drink of orange juice and batted my eyes at Nadine.

"Tessa blames this on you," Nadine said. "She blames all this shit on you. Said Sven had never even come home drunk before he met you." Her voice was cold. Lola was at the table too, eating pancakes, her feet swinging off the chair. Her plate was awash in maple syrup, the pancakes floating like lily pads.

"Lola!" Nadine said. "Get your bag ready and go to the car, okay, honey? I'll be there in a second." She leaned in low beside my face and I looked down. Our story had done its work, but I knew how far I had fallen. Lola squirmed down below the table and ran off to her bedroom, her face sticky with syrup and butter.

"Anyway, you're done with all that, aren't you?" Nadine hissed. "You hear me? Done. *Grow up.*"

And then, so much worse, and whispered even quieter: "Be a man."

Knockout.

She'd swung from her heels and broken my jaw. And down went Lily. Down went Lily.

The house was empty after she slammed the door, so I went to the couch with a glass of orange juice and flipped channels, my belly sour, my face sore. Even a pillow hurt. The telephone rang and I let the machine answer it. It was Sven, but I didn't know what to say anymore. I knew our time had come.

"Hey, it's Sven. Look, I just want to say how sorry I am about everything last night. I hope you're all right. Nadine told Tessa that your nose wasn't broken too badly and that it won't look bad forever. Anyway, I just wanted to let you guys know that I'm looking forward to those five boxes of Thin Mints. I'll be over there later to pick them up. Take it easy. Bye."

Sven was good people. Through and through good people. Decent and square. But I was too. I was good people too, and I was taking it all on my chin. Nadine was pissed. Tessa was pissed. And I was losing my best friend. Not because I had necked with a Russian ballerina in the bathroom of some country bumpkin bar, but because Sven had, and was either too smart or too dumb to get his skinny ass out of the bind.

I stood up from the couch and went to the refrigerator. It was nine o clock in the morning, but I decided to have a beer and lick my wounds. The orange juice was a nice chaser to the beer and I drank like that until lunch, when I was hungry and found the cases of Girl Scout Cookies in the basement and carried them up to the couch, where I stationed myself in front of the television, eating until I could not eat more, opening up box after box, and deciding that Thin Mints were my favorite. For the second time in twenty-four hours, I passed out with the television screen before me, aglow with happy faces, happy for another Today in New York City.

The doorbell rang and I was covered in the crumbs of my daughter's cookies. I rubbed my eyes, shut off the TV, and went to the door. It was Sven. Black-eyed and broken-lipped, his throat garishly decorated in a chain of bruises, he craned his face to look down at me and I could see there was real sadness there. Sven was my friend and I could see that he understood that we were done.

"Come in," I said. "Want a beer?"

"Why not," he said. "Could be the last one, the way Tessa ripped into Nadine last night. Oh, and I got a check for Lola's cookies." He handed me a check and I put it underneath a magnet on the humming refrigerator.

"Yeah," I said. "I'm in the doghouse for sure on this one. How's the eye?"

"You got any ice?" he asked.

So we sat that way until five, by which point Nadine might be home with Lola from day care, Sven holding a bag of frozen broccoli on his face, both of us drinking beer and eating Girl Scout Cookies in silence, just the sound of our jaws working.

"I'm so sorry," he said.

"It's all right, things'll cool down. You know how these things are. They're upset."

"I know, but it's my fault. Not yours. It was me in there with that girl, not you."

"Yeah, but I left you. And I took us to that place to begin with."

I didn't know whose fault it was anymore, and maybe it didn't matter. The whole thing was so dumb and I was losing my best friend in the world for it.

He put his bottle up and drained the last dregs. "Come on, you didn't leave me," he said. "I just said that. That was all on me. That was on me, and I'm sorry. I shouldn't have done that because I didn't want or need it anyway. You know?"

I didn't understand at first, but then I did and I nodded and we stood up. I was acutely aware in that moment of our trajectories in life, and how Sven was like the NASA space shuttle, his path nearly a vertical stairway, a plume of thick white cotton smoke beneath him as he raced toward the sky. He was the only person I'd ever met who could've been an astronaut; he was that good.

"Take it easy, Sven," I said, clasping his forearm, which fit like a broom handle between my fingers.

"Take it easy, Lily," he said, slouching down to hug me, his little pit bull.

MORELS

The best piece of advice that I ever had
Never go to church with blood on your hands.
—Charlie Parr

THE THREE MEN MOVED OVER the south-facing slopes above the valleys, their faces low to the ground, eyes sweeping the forest floor like midday searchlights. Their pursed lips clamped joints of marijuana, and over their shoulders their smoke went like the thick white whiskers of a beard in vain neglect. Bathed in the tang of the smoke, they wet their lips occasionally with bottles of beer that they carried through the forest in a heavy backpack, the bottles a set of oddly muted chimes.

"Too early," said Rimes. "Too goddamn early. Hard frost last night. That's no damn good."

"They're going to be popping," said Coffee confidently. "They're gonna start popping and we'll be right on top of 'em when they do."

"I'd like to see that," said Deere. "I want to see 'em come out of the earth. You think anyone's ever done that before? Like one of those time-elapsed movies of clouds moving or something?"

Rimes and Coffee ignored Deere, whose eyelids drooped heavily over his dull and dilated pupils.

The elm trees were champagne flutes cracked black against the sky, and they went to those dead trees and hovered around the trunks, where the bark peeled off in great scabs. The apple trees not yet softened with white-pink blossoms were craggy and lichened, stingy with their buds, and the men congregated beneath those trees too. They walked everywhere together, a band of stoned foragers, carrying their mesh bags of morels. When one man stopped to roll a joint, the others stopped too, and he would roll each man a fat cigarette. When one man stopped and dropped his pants to his ankles, the other two would do likewise, and they might be seen, backs to one another, urinating into the forest as if their counterparts were invisible strangers.

Not yet noon the day had grown hot. They removed their sweaters and Deere stripped off all his shirts and went about the forest like an animal clothed only in pants and boots. His body was ethereally white and he seemed to glow as he wobbled clumsily around, dimly observing the world through his own kaleidoscopic perspective.

"I'll take another beer," said Rimes to Coffee, who reached over his own shoulder into the bag of bottles and produced two, one that he passed to Rimes and the other that he raised to his own lips. They tapped bottles and made a small noise. They watched Deere and shook their heads.

"Stoned out of his dome," said Rimes.

"Tell you what," said Coffee. "You get that man out of his suit and tie and he loses his fucking mind."

Deere worked in electronic security. When he explained to Rimes and Coffee the inner machinations of his workday, he could see their eyes glaze over in confusion and he understood. He lived in a make-believe world of numbers and letters and electronic pulses and at his office he rarely saw women or talked to other men in conversations that were not monosyllabic or socially awkward. So when Deere found himself in the woods with Rimes and Coffee, he let loose and the other two men obliged him, guarded over him, even. Coffee had herbal tea in his truck to hide the traces of Deere's marijuana binges. Deere had the kind of employer who paid well but insisted on quarterly urine samples.

"How much we got?" asked Rimes, mopping his forehead as he marked the progress of the rising sun.

"Maybe a pound and a half," Coffee said. "Not much considering we been out all morning."

"Well," said Rimes, "my vote is we go find a bar, eat some lunch, have some beers, and come back midafternoon when these damn things start popping."

"I won't argue with that," said Coffee.

"Hey, Deere!" yelled Rimes.

Deere turned to his friends from the bird's nest he'd been

examining with some melancholy in the low-hanging branches of a nearby apple tree.

"Goddamn eggs are blue as the sky," reported Deere, shaking his head in wonder. "Baby blue." He walked toward Rimes and Coffee and then past the two men, down the hill and toward their camp and vehicles. "Somebody put some food in my gullet," he said without turning back to look at his friends. "I'm famished."

Rimes and Coffee looked at each other and smiled.

They had all grown up in those unglaciated hills; that part of the world left intact by the last glaciers that steamrolled the surrounding land, leaving it utterly flat. The Driftless Area, like a postcard of what had been. It was a place on earth unlike anywhere else, and as children they had merely used it as a playground, a place to swim or hunt or build their secret forts. They built faulty rafts to float the rivers and streams and stalked the forest creatures to test their own stealth. As children they had run together like their own small clan, learning the caves, coulees, draws, hollows, and springs bubbling up out of the planet like a good wound, giving up the coldest, sweetest water.

Deere had left for the city and started into computers at the right time and before almost anyone else. He'd done well for himself, with a big house in the suburbs. He had married, which surprised Rimes and Coffee when it happened and they were called to his side in a great urban cathedral to be his groomsmen. As a child, Deere had been the smallest and skinniest of them all, and he wept when the other two boys outran him or hid from him among the sumac or deep inside a cave. He had failed as an athlete, been terrified of girls. But then one day he was a man, their friend, more successful than anyone they'd ever known, with a beautiful wife who had the look in her eye of a woman deeply in love with a decent man who saw only her and no one else in the whole world. Deere's marriage had stunned Rimes and Coffee, and they had drawn into themselves, into each other, becoming not unlike circus Siamese twins sharing a torso and limbs. With Deere off and married and out of their world, they lived within the hills, two loud coyotes running from bar to bar, chasing women, wrecking trucks, wasting motorcycles. At the end of their evenings they built fires on the banks of the river and stared into the flames, looking for things they didn't know.

Deere was so stoned he passed out in the bed of Coffee's truck before his friends reached the base of the hill. His skin, pale as milk only six hours ago, had darkened to an angry pink.

"Deere!" yelled Rimes as he slapped the side of the truck. "Put on a goddamned shirt, man. We're going to a nice establishment." He threw his friend a T-shirt and Deere slid it on, wincing, then promptly fell back to sleep.

Rimes and Coffee slid onto the bench seat of the truck and pulled out, winding through the valley bottoms. In the fields, sandhill cranes stabbed at the black earth and the yellow stubble of cornstalks, leftovers of the autumn harvest.

"There was a time people shot those birds," said Rimes.

Coffee shook his head. "Lucky there's anything left of anything, the way people are."

The hills had emptied of people like them, and Rimes and Coffee knew it. Old men who'd run general stores for decades were dying, leaving their shelves empty, their doors unlocked. The children of those entrepreneurs taped FOR SALE signs in the windows and then left. Those buildings stayed vacant and then other buildings went vacant until whole communities came to a standstill, as if something had come silently through and sucked the breath of life away, leaving only the husks of a former time. In the newspaper stands long ignored, stories now years old moldered into history.

And yet even as the towns themselves hollowed out, the hills and coulees were being resettled. The Amish had found the Driftless, all the farms without farmers, barns without cows, and they had come out on their horse-drawn buggies and bought things up. But they were like a thing apart and unto themselves, moving around the area in a loud silence, all in black, always somber. So the hills were gaining people quietly, mute new inhabitants whose language seemed to be labor and prayer.

Coffee and Rimes had hung on, two outliers, two stones too stubborn to erode away. Rimes the tractor and seed salesman and Coffee the marijuana farmer. Rimes had bought his parents' old home while Coffee lived in a small Airstream at the nape of a lost coulee, a nowhere geography not easily photographed by passing airplanes or satellites.

"Where to then?" asked Coffee.

"Let's hit up the Antlers," said Rimes. "They got good burgers."

Coffee nodded his head and peered over his shoulder at their slumbering friend, his lips moving in some secret, nonsensical language.

The Antlers was a low bunker of a bar, dark and festooned everywhere with taxidermy, much of it from a time when animals populated the draws and coulees in greater numbers. The walls were sharp with great baskets of antlers, and below the American ivory were glistening eyes like minor stars that held the light of the pastel glow of the jukebox.

Poachers sat at the bar, bags of mushrooms at the feet of their stools, heavy and fragrant with the earth and the specific rot found beneath a dense carpet of leaves. The three men sat at the bar, Deere unsteady on his stool, Coffee and Rimes seated close beside him, holding Deere to the planet he threatened to spill off of.

"Three beers and three burgers," said Coffee to the bartender, a woman named Trixie whose son had been lost in Iraq, a contractor who drove jet fuel through the desert. His high school graduation photo in an ornate frame near the cash register.

The beer came first, and Coffee and Rimes downed it lustily, the apples in their throats working like thirsty pumps.

Deere bobbed and weaved on his stool, his eyes jacketed behind heavy lids.

"Where are we?" he asked.

"The Antlers," said Rimes as Trixie deftly delivered their plates onto the counter in front of their resting elbows and dirty hands.

"Looks like a zoo," slurred Deere. "A zoo full of dead things."

"Taxidermy." Rimes laughed. "Eat that burger now, the mushrooms are going to start to pop."

"Zoos make me sad," said Deere as he picked the burger off its paper plate and opened his mouth slowly, hugely, before deciding he needed to finish the thought. "Just a damn jail. A jail for animals. No better than going to a jail and poking at the inmates. Throwing food at them. Getcha fuckin' killed." Suddenly he Frisbeed a hamburger bun at the frozen bust of a sixteen-point buck.

The poachers at the bar were staring down the rail at Deere, and Trixie's arms were folded tightly near the cash register, where behind her the lost son smiled broadly, his haircut already slightly dated.

"Eat that burger," ordered Coffee. "Eat that burger and sober up and be halfways good, for chrissakes. Maybe we can get out of here before somebody tries to kill you."

"Fuck 'em," said Deere, his mouth full of meat and dripping grease. "I'm ready."

"Check, please," said Coffee, offering Trixie a tight-lipped, handsome smile.

"Sober him up," she said as she handed him the bill. "Sober him up 'fore he says something stupid. It's too early for that philosophical shit anyway. Hard to believe he come from here at all."

Coffee paused. Looked at her hard to let her know that Deere was still his friend. Conveying to her that they were bonded just as brothers are or the strangle molecules that hold the rain together or the particles of a boulder.

"He's as much this place as anyone else and probably a good goddamned deal better than any of us," said Coffee quietly to Trixie in a tone and volume meant for her only. "And he's my goddamned friend. And we'll sit here all fucking day and drink your beer if we so choose."

He brought the wad of bills down on the bar inside a knuckled fist, his thick hand making a crack like a walnut detonating into fragments. It stilled the bar, turned the poachers' faces down, where they stared at the bubbles rising in their beer glasses. Trixie's eyes flitted to the crumpled money, twice what their bill had been, and she lowered her head too, pretended to survey her toenails, which needed a new coat of paint. Coffee never took his eyes off her. Trixie acted tough at the Antlers, but Coffee knew her from all around and knew that she was mostly broken by her son's death, and sometimes when she came down his driveway in an ancient Bronco with a younger girlfriend looking to buy pot, he would invite them into his trailer and they would smoke together in a tight circle where he could watch as her sorrow lifted or faded like the early evening sun becoming night. He knew the money he'd just left on the bar would come back to him, but he always wished it wouldn't and that she might just move on to someplace else.

"Come on, Deere," said Coffee, lifting his friend from the stool. "Let's get us some morels." He shot a glance at Rimes, who nodded as they lifted Deere's arms over their shoulders and shrugged him out of the bar, carrying their friend, the walking wounded, stoned and drunk, back into the daylight just as the sun found its zenith in an unblemished sky.

"Let's get him to drink some water," said Rimes. "I got a canteen somewhere."

"Beer is water!" said Deere loudly to no one in particular. Then, quieter, "Beer is water."

Rimes found the canteen behind the bench seat and, unscrewing the cap, took a small sip before holding the vessel to his friend's parched lips.

"Artesian water," said Rimes.

Deere nursed the canteen greedily and finished its contents, burping into his hand and wiping his lips. He seemed instantly more sober.

"I tell you what," he said, his voice already more steady, "that's a whole lot better'n city water. The stuff back home? Tastes like pool water and cleaning products. I can barely drink it. Even my ice cubes smell funny." He shook his head. "Artesian water, huh?" He looked at Rimes admiringly.

"Right out of the earth," said Rimes. "Best thing in the world. Cold and sweet and free."

"I'd like to find an artesian beer spring," said Deere,

imagining his Big Rock Candy Mountain. "All the free beer a guy could drink. What do you think of that?"

They laughed and Coffee slapped Deere on the back, causing him to wince, his sunburn now a suit of pain.

"Daniel Deere has risen from the dead," said Coffee happily.

"All right, then," said Deere. "Let's go find some fucking morels."

And so all three men piled onto the bench seat of the truck, their favorite pew, and the truck carried them away from the Antlers full of food and newly revived. On the radio was an old Merle Haggard song, and inside the car they beat their fists against whatever halfway flat surface they could reach, and through the countryside the truck went, a motley kind of percussion section accompanied by a trio of happy voices as the men sang together, butchering the lyrics but always perfectly synchronized on the refrain. Their bellies were full and they felt invincible and high and an unlikely family only occasionally reunited.

The truck pulled to a stop beside a steeply inclined hill that rose into a sharp nipple in the sky, its slopes everywhere studded by dead elms.

"Got the beers?" asked Deere.

"Got 'em," said Coffee.

"Got the weed?" asked Deere.

Coffee patted his breast pocket. "My man," he said. "We got enough weed to get a buffalo high. Now, you ready, or you need another fuckin' catnap?"

Deere smiled. "I know those mushrooms are popping now. You can damn near hear 'em if you just try." Deere did not smoke either cigarettes or marijuana usually, but he did in the company of Rimes and Coffee. "Let's make hay," he said, lighting a joint and beginning to storm the hill.

The mushrooms were indeed popping now. Everywhere beneath the elms they emerged from the earth, their form a dunce cap textured like brain, just slightly harder than cottage cheese. Beneath the trees the men went on their hands and knees, careful not to disrupt the forest floor too much, knives in hands, cutting the mushrooms free of their bases, stuffing the morels into their bags. They did not shout upon discovering a cache of mushrooms. There were other men in the forests too, and voices carried between the hillsides, through the valleys. So the three friends just whistled low to one another, always careful to stay close, their whistles like the call of a strange new bird, their own flock of three.

At dusk they stopped.

"How much we got?" Deere asked excitedly.

They emptied bag after bag into the trunk of Coffee's truck and surveyed the bounty as they sipped beers.

"Must be twelve, fifteen pounds," said Rimes, shaking his head in wonder. "A good goddamned day is what I have to say about it all."

The three men shook hands and grinned widely. They were filled with a kind of glow, warm and big in their chests.

"You ought to take all these mushrooms back for your wife," Coffee said to Deere. Rimes looked up, mildly aghast.

"The hell are we gonna do with fifteen pounds of morels?" Deere laughed. "Shit. I love Diane too, but mostly we eat out anyway."

"Still," continued Coffee, "you could show her what we do together. What it's like to live up here. What you're capable of finding for free just walking around the woods. Shit, you two could walk into any fancy restaurant down there and probably sell these mushrooms for three, four hundred dollars."

"Well, we're doing just fine," Deere said casually. "We don't need the money. Maybe you two oughta split the takings. I don't mind. Leave me enough for an omelet or something."

A look of subdued hurt streaked quickly across Coffee's face, the celebration of only a moment earlier abruptly extinguished. Deere seemed to flinch too, perhaps recognizing in the after-moment just how different their lives were. Here his friend had been trying to give a nearly priceless ephemeral gift, and he had turned it to ash.

Rimes saw their glows fading and spoke up. "You know what I think. I say we go back to my place, fry up a couple pans of these fuckers, grill some steaks, and hit the bars tonight. We can rehydrate, build a little base in our stomachs, maybe chase some tail, what do you think?"

With some relief Deere said, "Sounds good to me. Let me drive, though, huh? I never get to drive a pickup anymore, least of all on these roads. Crack me a beer, Coffee."

Deere had already moved behind the great loose wheel

of Coffee's pickup truck as the man reached into a heavily dented cooler to produce the last three bottles of beer, only now the slightest bit warm. Coffee didn't like money. Didn't like to talk about it, didn't even like the transactions of his business. Some nights in his Airstream, alone with the stars or the static of the radio, he thought about his measure as a man, the stock a stranger might take in him. He was more than what he seemed, but there were times in which he knew no better way of displaying himself than by flashing a fat roll of bills at the bar, yet in those moments he felt dry and shallow too. Deere's success intimidated him, the kind of wealth that opened worlds and people and knowledge that Coffee could not fathom. Deere's life was an unknowable and elegant charade to Coffee.

They all drank as the truck weaved over the road, stitching a jagged path between the painted lines, the headlights illuminating the marble eyes of animals along the way. Coffee let the money talk recede from his consciousness and relaxed against the bench seat, enjoying being chauffeured about the countryside. His eyelids closed and he eased into a light sleep, a faint smile easing across his face.

"Deere!" screamed Rimes suddenly. Coffee's eyes flashed open. He braced his thick arms against the dashboard.

What filled Deere's head in that instant was confusion as he turned his face away from the road to look at the horrified Rimes. He had thought Rimes was trying to say, "Deer!", but the driver of the drunken pickup saw no deer, and in turning to observe Rimes, he neglected to see the blaze orange reflective triangle affixed to the rear of a horse-drawn buggy. And so Coffee's truck hurtled straight into the buggy and smashed through its wood and metal skeleton until it was driving into and over the terrified horse, the animal letting out the stark, anguished scream of a creature losing its life in the night. The horse was clipped at its legs and its muscular body went flying into the darkness of the passenger-side ditch, limbs contorted sickly, the sheen of sweat on its glossy coat vibrant in the headlights, contours of bulging sinew and skin and bone, a beautiful thing wasted.

Blood on the cracked windshield, and the hood crumpled into a shallow U of steel. Deere hit the brakes and the tires skidded unbearably over the strange fluids now spilled all over the asphalt. And then they were still.

Deere began screaming and soon was hyperventilating, his breaths ragged and phlegmy with shock and confusion. Rimes grabbed Deere by the head and held him, wrapped him in his arms and held him and shushed him as if he were a man reversed into a baby.

Coffee kicked his mangled door free and moved into the night. He could hear the blood in the horse's lungs and the sound of its useless legs quivering in the night and it was almost more than his mind could process. For a moment his resolution was broken and he spun under the stars in a state of disbelief, all his nerves undone and burnt into a circuit of dead sensors.

The headlights were flickering and unreliable, splashed in red, so he moved blind in the night, using his feet to feel the debris and his ears to reach out into the black for any-thing that moved or spoke or cried. His feet touched the shredded canvas of the buggy's body. His feet tripped on the crippled metal chassis, then were caught in the leg trap of a broken wheel, its spokes gone in places. His feet kicked what he thought was a bag of clothing or food, and he reached down and instead touched the smooth face of a child. He jerked his hand back toward his own mouth, but his breath was gone. He knelt down slowly and touched the child again and knew the body was horribly still. He began moving back toward Deere's sobbing.

"Does it run?" he barked, not even waiting for a response. "Does the motherfucker run!"

"Christ, Coffee," said Rimes. "I mean, Jesus Christ is anyone out there?"

Coffee put his hand past Deere and touched the keys. The engine inexplicably was still running, ticking now loud against the night. Coffee pushed Deere toward the center of the bench, and though he could not see Rimes, he knew the man's face was etched in sorrow and confusion. Deere continued to babble and sing out bursts of unintelligible madness.

"Shut that door if you can," ordered Coffee. "Shut that fucking door and help me out here, Rimes. We've got to get him out of here. We've all got to go."

"What about the Amish?" said Rimes. "Are they out there?"

"It's done," said Coffee. "Jesus Christ, man, it is done. All I know is we got to get the fuck outta here, right now."

And then a thin wrecked voice called out, weak against the sound of the engine, and it said, "Help."

"Goddamn it, Coffee," said Rimes. "We get 'em and drop 'em in town, for God's sake. We can't leave 'em to die."

Deere wailed, his face a dripping mask of tears and snot.

"We're letting them be," said Coffee, and he closed his door and eased the truck limping forward and away from the unseen array of carnage.

In the morning, they pushed the truck into the river that bisected Coffee's land, and it sunk into the brown water and vanished. Rimes built a fire and burned their clothes in a pyre. They stared skittishly at the smudgy smoke that went up out over the coulee. Afterward, Deere just rocked himself back and forth on Coffee's couch. His face was swollen, his eyes red and haunted. Coffee tuned the radio, searching for news of the crash, but when he found it, turned the volume down so that only he could learn the details. The police were searching for the killers of a small boy, criminals who had crippled a family and killed their horse. Coffee turned the radio off and watched the embers of their fire.

"Let me make a call," he said aloud and to no one in particular. "Get us another vehicle." Then, "Rimes, call Deere's wife and make some shit up. We all need an alibi. I'll call Trixie and call in a favor."

Rimes nodded his head and stared at Deere, still rocking back and forth, like a man who had dropped his faculties all the way down a very deep, dark well.

They spent the day on Coffee's land, barely moving at all. They drank tea and artesian water. From time to time Deere went outside to stand beside the smoldering remains of their garments. He threw stones into the water. His friends watched him like a man on suicide watch.

Coffee smoked a cigarette. He looked at Rimes in a hard way and said, "I've been in worse spots than this. We'll get it figured."

When he came out of it, the first thing Deere asked was "Where's their church?"

"This is real life, Daniel," Rimes said. "Okay? Coffee'll take you home to your wife, but then . . . You can never come back here."

Deere looked into Rimes's eyes. "There has to be a service. Someone got killed."

Coffee shook his head, looking out at the river where the truck now rested under twelve feet of murky water. "They don't have churches," he said. "It'll be at a house. The family's house, probably. Christ, Deere, come on."

"Daniel, just stay away from this," Rimes said. "They're looking for a long-haul truck driver. We play this smart, it just goes away." He made a motion with his hand, as if to smooth the air between them.

"No," said Deere. "I own this thing. I killed someone. I fucking killed someone."

Coffee shook his head, ran his hands over his unshaven face.

"Goddamnit, Daniel, stay away from this!" snapped Rimes, standing from his chair to loom up over his seated friend.

"I'm not a fucking kid!" said Deere. "Okay, Rimes! And listen, don't you fucking worry. I'm not going to squeal on you."

The house was a tall, rambling affair, a white building on a hill, and they knew that it was the one from the multitude of horses and buggies outside. Coffee pulled Trixie's Bronco to the margin of the gravel road a quarter mile from the house. He shut off the engine and looked out at the stark structure. Rimes was back to work. It was just Deere and Coffee. Glancing across the vehicle at his friend, Coffee saw that the man had lost weight in just the few days since the accident and that in patches, his hair seemed to have lost its color and gone white.

"I'll tell you again," Coffee said, "I'll take you to Canada. Shit, I'd drive you to Mexico. Come on, Deere. You don't have to take all of this."

Deere shook his head.

"Then I'm calling my lawyer for you," said Coffee. "Christ. Christ, Daniel."

They parked the Bronco and walked the last hundred yards or so to the house.

Even before they came close to the house, they could hear the singing inside. They neared a bank of rectangular windows, careful not to be seen, pressing their backs to the wood clapboards of the building. The hymn came out of the mourners from a low place and went into the air like a bank of clouds. Deere moved closer to the window, positioning himself so he could see. Their backs were straight and their clothes were a darkness clinging to their skinny bodies. The men wore beards, though their upper lips were freshly shaved and ruddy in the cool air. The words were in another language, and Deere and Coffee stood outside of the house and listened and listened, and by and by Deere began silently crying and Coffee put his arm around his friend, held him. Their breaths were on the window of the house and created a gray fog.

A small body lay in repose at the front of a large room, and the face of the small body belonged to a little boy with blond hair. His hair captured what little light entered the building like fibers of good energy. A coffin was near his body on the floor, and outside the house Coffee thought he smelled freshly cut pine.

The two men stood outside of the assembly for some time, hardly breathing. Deere had come to pay his respects, but now he was like a ghost just outside the building, watching the dead boy and his people. Deere weeping silently.

Coffee leaned into his friend. "Deere, I have to have a smoke. Come with me."

Deere remained frozen, his body stiff, his color gone, his cheeks wet where the tears had been.

Coffee touched Deere's elbow. "Come on, just a cigarette."

They moved quietly away from the house and back down the gravel road, and Coffee began walking back toward the Bronco. He lighted a cigarette and rubbed his temples with the rough padding of his fingers.

"Let's go for a drive," he said over his shoulder. Deere moved into the Bronco cautiously, as if it were a trap. Coffee turned the engine over and backed away from the house, and then headed on down a hillside and into a draw of yellow sandstone, where patches of moss clung to the rock, remaining green all year long. They wound their way through a valley, and when they came to the town's only intersection, Coffee could see that Deere was looking toward the antique streetlights of the old police station, a small square of a brick building with a single cell. Coffee flashed the left directional and they turned southeast, away from the town, away from all of it.

"Where are we going?" said Deere, his question unconvincing.

They did not talk. Just marked the herds of deer and the cows resting out in the fields in the warm afternoon mud. They drove past the abandoned farms, the windmills turning fruitlessly and conjuring no energy or water, past cemeteries long ignored and junkyards where dogs ran from behind chain link fences to chase Trixie's SUV down the road.

Once outside of the place that had formed them, they

stopped at a gas station and filled Styrofoam cups with burnt-tasting coffee. Coffee leaned against the muddy Bronco as he pumped gasoline and looked out over the land, which was noticeably flatter here and everywhere covered by fields of corn in tight lines that showed the contours of the planet as neatly as a topographic map.

"I don't want to go to jail," Deere said. "It was an accident."

Coffee nodded. "I know."

They drove slowly, watching the telephone lines crest and fall from pole to pole, not a few of them capped with hawks looking out over the yellow plain. And then the telephone lines converged with great high-tension power lines, and from the state line south they watched as energy ran in rivers of cable toward the city, cables of electricity and power in concentrations so vast that when they rolled down their windows, the atmosphere seemed to vibrate with commerce, with information.

Coffee hated the taste of the city in his mouth, the thick sour air and the layers of brown in the sky that obscured the sun but also made the sunset before them almost apocalyptically beautiful in its intensity, so magenta and pink and orange that in the west the world seemed already destroyed.

"I'm not coming back," said Deere.

Coffee lighted a cigarette and nodded. "No, Daniel, you're not."

Deere's house was at the end of a cul-de-sac, and when they pulled into the driveway his wife stood illuminated in the headlights. She waved weakly. The house was lit like a cathedral, every window ablaze in yellows and creams and whites, and in the three-stall garage were two new vehicles, both gleaming under the light of a naked bulb. Deere's wife walked over to the passenger side of the Bronco, and Coffee could see that her eyes were red and puffy, dark bags sagging above her high cheekbones. She could not have known everything, but she knew something.

"Hello, Chuck," she said to Coffee, not unpleasantly. He remembered their wedding, when he had shared a dance with her, Diane's elegant body in his hands, fragile as Fabergé. The only other time he had ever slow-danced with a woman was back at their high school prom. Diane told him that night, "I shouldn't say this, but Daniel really looks up to you. He'd follow you anywhere. You know that, don't you?"

He had chosen to forget her words, and had, too, until that moment in their driveway, the Bronco still idling, her hand now inside the vehicle, resting on her husband's shoulder. Deere was home.

"Won't you come in, Chuck," Diane said. "I'll make you a cup of tea or I can fix you something for dinner. You look beat."

Coffee smiled in a very tired sort of way. "I wish that I could, Di."

He looked out at his friend's neighborhood. The cul-de-sac a horseshoe of miniature mansions, all bright with incandescent light, each lawn a carefully cut emerald. He extended his hand to Deere and they shook. Then Deere released the latch of his seat belt and slid out of the vehicle.

"I'll send down some more mushrooms," Coffee said. "Daniel forgot his back at my place."

Diane looked at her husband and then at Coffee, this time much more warily. "I don't know that Daniel has ever come back with mushrooms. Makes a girl wonder what you three are up to."

Coffee and Deere smiled and Coffee released the brake and rolled down the minor slope of their driveway. He waved as he put the Bronco into drive and aimed the vehicle north.

The butter had all melted in the pan when Coffee added the onions and garlic and then the mushrooms. Immediately the kitchen was dense with the smell of rich earth. A joint smoldered in an ashtray near the hot plate and the tang of the weed was sharp, its bitterness softened by the citric sweetness of hops or maybe lemongrass. It was a week since the accident. Coffee had been lying low, staying close to his coulee and never answering the old rotary telephone near his bed. He had not seen Rimes since before the boy's funeral. In the newspapers, the investigation was already slowing.

He saw the police cruiser as it moved slowly up his driveway and took a final drag from the marijuana cigarette before throwing it into the toilet and flushing. He dripped a drop of saline in each eye, moved the mushrooms off the hot plate, and went outside to intercept his visitor.

"Charles," said the officer, who had known Coffee's parents. They shook hands.

"I just cooked up some morels," offered Coffee gamely. "Help me eat them before they go cold."

"All right," said the officer as he removed his hat.

The Airstream was tight with Coffee's books, DVDs, and television, and from the walls hung posters of famous paintings and early maps of the unglaciated region. The air inside the trailer was unmistakable, and Coffee propped open a window.

They sat at Coffee's only table, a tiny rectangle, and ate from the pan with separate forks.

"Goddamn," said the officer appreciatively.

"I know it," said Coffee. "All that butter finds those chambers of the mushrooms and coats everything."

The officer shook his head and collected himself. "Shame about those Amish," he said.

Coffee nodded his head but remained silent, and they sat that way until they both looked out the window, to the river, where the waters had dropped after all the upstate snow had melted away. The water was less turbid, and Coffee knew that in a week the skeleton of the truck might be visible at the bottom of the river.

"Is there something I can do to help you, Officer?" asked Coffee, leaning back in his chair.

"Actually," said the older man, "there is." He scratched the top of his head, where the hair was growing thin. Long blond strands stretched from one ear to the other over the pale, glossy scalp of the policeman. He reached under the table and produced his wallet, which was full of fifty-dollar bills. He set the thick wallet down on the table so the corners of the bills were fanned out just slightly.

"My ma has the glaucoma," he said. "And, well, she sent me here because she heard you were the man to talk to."

Coffee inhaled slowly, paused. "Your mom is in some pain?"

"She's in a good deal of pain," said the officer.

Coffee nodded and stood, selected three books off his shelf, opening them to reveal three clear zippered bags full of marijuana. He placed them on the table, and the officer looked over them as he chewed his mushrooms and scratched his head. Coffee rolled two new joints and lighted both cigarettes in his mouth. He passed one to the older man, who examined the joint with some uncertainty before slowly inhaling a great cloud of smoke. He held it inside his lungs for a long time, and then exhaled in a groan, the muscles in his face relaxing until his skin hung in jowls off his jawline, and his lips stretched into a smile.

Coffee looked out the window again, through the gauze of the smoke to the river, and he said, "I'm sorry to hear about your mother."

LEFTOVERS

_____

KNEELING, NECK-DEEP IN THE REFRIGERATOR, white light suffusing her face, she tosses his mother's food into a black garbage bag beside her. He stands at the Formica countertop, watching her wrapping dishes and utensils in newspaper. The house is so quiet. All the radios and televisions are gone. Most of the rooms so barren they echo.

"I count six bottles of mustard," Renée says. "And butter. Eight sticks in here and four boxes in the freezer." _Four boxes._ She lived by herself. Did she put butter in everything?

Renée wears elbow-length yellow rubber gloves, constantly swipes strands of hair away from her face. Blows at them angrily, as if they were mosquitoes, wasps.

Mason walks two boxes out to the trunk of their car. He breathes deeply. His mother had never quite approved of Renée, would've screamed to find her there in the kitchen, scrutinizing the contents of her refrigerator. He never understood it, how they could dislike each other so politely, so quietly, so instinctually. And Renée, equally obstinate about his mother. Renée had hated his mother's "fashion," her interior decorating, her taste in fiction, her cooking. Hated it. All of it.

A salad, she would say, can't we mix in a salad? Just for fun? Like an experiment?

He returns to the kitchen with more newspaper, more boxes. Steadily they are emptying the house out. Their work is almost complete. Only the garage is left, its dirty rags and motor oil and tools and the deflated footballs and basketballs of his youth. Already they have filled a Dumpster with her things. The dusty furniture, the sun-bleached wall hangings, the knickknacks, old socks, old underwear. It was Mason who had gone through her clothing. Renée refused. He had thrown out her silk stockings, her brassieres, her tented camisoles. Dispossessed the wire hangers of their clothing. Cleared out her dresser drawers, those things she had worn, many of the garments mended and remended. The cotton worn so thin, it seemed a gauze. He looked for her wedding dress but never found it.

"I'm just going to throw these leftovers away," Renée says. "I mean, this is disgusting."

His mother cooked rich food. Mason loved her cooking. Even after leaving home and traveling the world. After marrying Renée, after losing twenty pounds and never regaining it. Still. Cold winter nights he thinks about her lasagna. Her cassoulet. Her chili. Her pâté. Her Bolognese.

Her fresh bread. The butter dish. Ice cream and pie and cobbler. The nights he and Renée came to visit his mother, how ravenously he'd shovel food into his mouth, taking seconds, wiping grease and olive oil off the plate with sliced bread. His mother heaping food onto his plate, smiling, feeding him, nourishing him in this way. Renée across the table, politely nibbling, pushing parcels of food around her plate as if her dish had been poisoned. Smiling grimly.

Standing over the sink, wrapping coffee mugs emblazoned with the names of places his mother visited in her retirement—*Branson, Gatlinburg, Galena, Wisconsin Dells*—he thinks about nights there, Sunday nights when he might leave Renée at home and come visit his mother. A bouquet of sunflowers in his hand.

There's a lightbulb out in that hallway, his mother would say, I'm scared of ladders these days.

Or,

The toilet is always running. Keeps me up nights. Would you mind looking at it?

His mother boiling noodles, steam collecting into droplets on her eyelashes. His mother wrapping leftovers in aluminum foil, handing the food to him like a package, saying, Here, bring some home for Renée. Tell her I missed seeing her.

Renée, who *loathes* leftovers. Who leaves doggy bags and cardboard boxes on restaurant tables for waiters to rush after them screaming, You forgot your food! Renée, reaching for those leftovers as if the container were a bomb she had left there, its timer counting down to *0:00*.

He can't remember the last time they made love. It has become a memory game, recalling that occasion. Sometimes, even when they are together, perhaps at the grocery store or riding in an airplane, he will close his eyes feigning sleep and think, *Has it been a year? Two? Three?*

They don't talk to each other anymore. At least not substantively. Financially they are comfortable, and money is no longer even an entrée into conflict. She plays bridge three nights a week. He is on a bowling league, plays softball with a lineup of other older guys. The only thing they have left are movies. They drive to a multiplex beside the highway. Sometimes they don't even see the same film. When they do, they rarely speak before the show or after. He works a sudoku puzzle, she peers down at her cell. She falls asleep on the drive home. Sometimes he carries her into their bedroom, removes her shoes, pulls the quilts over her. He has heard her mumble, I love you, but can't remember when. Sometimes she asks that he leave her in the car to sleep.

One evening they disagreed so vehemently about a film that she would not talk to him for three days afterward. She banged around their house, slamming doors, rattling pots and pans.

How does a distance so wide open between two people

who live together so intimately? Who have loved each other? He can't explain it. Can't explain where the magic went, the love, the friendship, the decency, the partnership. He doesn't miss their sex. But he longs for her as a companion. A person to walk with, to hold hands with, to watch television with. To be happily silent with. He wonders if she feels the same, or if this rift is just something that has opened inside him.

A bad quiet envelops their marriage. Mason imagines a small-town telephone booth from which he calls her and waits for her voice. She answers, her voice like a very cold wind traveling through thousands of miles of telephone wire. Then she puts him on hold and he imagines her walking away forever, leaving him there, through all time, waiting for either a dial tone or a dead click. Neither of which ever come. He grows older in that telephone booth, so much older, until it becomes his glassy coffin.

"Miracle Whip," Renée says. "She had two of those. Wouldn't want to run out of Miracle Whip now, would we."

She throws the glass jars into the garbage bag.

Mason stops working and looks at her on her knees, the edges of her underwear peeking up and over the waist of her blue jeans. He feels something like lust rush over him and considers going over to her, fucking her, surprising her. Maybe that is exactly what they need. Maybe that is what she wants from him. To end their cold war. To collapse onto, against each other, for all their tension and anger to be broken loose.

But he is afraid. Afraid she'll scream, afraid she'll look at him like a madman, a rapist. And maybe that is what it would be. How can he even know anymore.

She stands up slowly, her hands pressed against the small of her back. He smiles at her. But his face feels stiff, his lips dumb, the muscles there frozen. Smiling, it seems to him, has become like a rainbow in wintertime. Not impossible, but implausible.

"I need a break," she says. "I need some fresh air."

He touches her shoulder and she starts, as if shocked. Looks at him coldly.

He could not have cleaned the house without her. His mother lived in this house alone for the last thirty years. She was not a hoarder exactly, but she did accumulate things. The attic was the worst. Mouse turds and choking dust and pink fiberglass insulation and sweltering heat and biting cold. Boxes of magazines, boxes of yarn, of Christmas lights and relics of Mason's childhood. Box by box they threw it all away. A two-person bucket brigade.

Renée never complained. He admires that about her. She is tough.

Last year Mason had a heart attack. It happened at the movies. All the telltale symptoms: the sweats, the lightning bolts of pain in his arm and chest. She knew right away.

"Hold still," she said evenly, "let me get help."

He was glad then for her telephone, which she used to call 9-1-1 while he sat, watching the opening credits of a film they would never finish.

She followed the ambulance rather than ride with him.

"Go on," he said, "I'll be okay. It just makes sense. Then we don't need a cab to come get the car."

She had stared at him.

He knows that what he should have said is *Please. I need you. Please come with me. I'm scared.*

In the ambulance an EMT said to him, "You're a lucky man. Your wife caught it quick. Most people aren't that lucky. A few minutes' difference and man, I tell you, you're a goner. And look at her back there. She's holding it down. Practical too. You guys thought to get your car."

Mason wept, his face falling apart. He did not make a sound. The EMT turned to him and said, "Man, you all right? You in pain? Let's get you some meds. Hold on, man. Stay with me, man. You're fine. We got you. We got you. Hang in there. I'm right here. Your wife is right there, man. I can see her. I can see your wife, man. She's follow-ing us. We're almost there."

He gets to his knees, peers into the refrigerator. Even after all of Renée's work, it is still full of food. Apples, carrots, cab-bage, cheese, milk, pickles, salad dressing, sour cream, whipped cream, yogurt . . . It looks like she was still feeding a family. Like she was ready for Renée and him to come over for a feast. That she was lonely for visitors, diners, mouths to feed.

He misses her. She knew he wasn't happy. Once she actually asked about his marriage. She put her hands on his face as if he were nine years old. Looked into his eyes until he could no longer look at her and aimed his eyes at her kitchen table.

She said, "Getting a divorce doesn't mean you failed. It just means you grew apart. Happens every day."

"You and Dad never got divorced," he said, still looking at the table.

"Oh, sweetie," she said, "your dad and I weren't happy for years."

"But I still love her," Mason said.

"I know you do, baby, I know that you do."

Renée returns to the kitchen. "I'm hungry," she says. "Let's go. We can come back tomorrow."

He lets his head sag. Feels the refrigerator's fan kick on, warm air hitting his knees, cold air against his face and neck. He is tired, lonely, heartsick.

"Come on," she says, "get up."

He can't look at her. "No," he says. "I'm going to stay here. There's food enough here."

He reaches for an orange Tupperware container in the back corner of the refrigerator. He peels off the top and the container seems to burp. Or sigh. It is cassoulet. He stands, carries the Tupperware to the microwave. Leans against the counter while the food heats. He looks at her.

"You know I won't eat that."

He nods.

"So what? So you want me to bring you back something? So you want to walk home? So what?"

The words are a reservoir; his teeth, his lips are the dam. He shakes his head, bites his lip.

"Mason?"

Inside the microwave, the food circles like a carousel. The light in there is strange.

"Mason?"

"I'm going to stay here," he says.

He owns the house now. Or they do. But already he's certain that he wants to live there the rest of his days. The microwave beeps three times loudly. He lets it beep; what is the hurry? Reaches for the Tupperware, and it is hot enough to burn his fingers, his palms, but he does not wince, won't give her that gift. Carries the Tupperware to the kitchen table where he has eaten hundreds, thousands of meals. Walks again across the kitchen. Gathers a fork. Pours himself a glass of whole milk. It is so opaque, so thick, so white.

"Mason, that food could be a week, two weeks old. Who knows? Are you all right? Mason?"

Her voice is rising.

He looks at her, says, "I'm so sorry." What he thinks is *I want a divorce.*

Then he forks a bite of beans, of duck, of sausage. Lifts it to his mouth, chews, swallows. He imagines his mother's hands preparing this food. His mother's mouth eating this same food. He imagines tasting her lipstick. Imagines her alone, sitting at the very table where he sits now.

He chews slowly, washes the food down with a swallow of milk. His throat pumps it all down.

"Mason," she says. "Mason, I'm your wife."

He shakes his head, says, "I'm sorry. I'm just so sorry."

BENEATH THE BONFIRE

Meant, I knew—of course I knew—
That it would be only a matter of weeks,
That there was nothing more to do.
—James Merrill, "Christmas Tree"

THEY WERE DRAGGING THE TREES across the frozen lake by their stumps, a trail of needles behind them, the crowns of the trees down against the ice, snow, and slush where once the apexes of the little trees had supported a brightly lit star or angel. Most of the trees had long since stopped drinking, the needles beginning to dot carpeting, the trees wrapped in lights and ornaments no longer gleeful, no longer merry, just combustible.

The tradition was to burn the trees out on the frozen lake on the first night of January. Kat watched as they marched out from shore, the trees making a low steady scratching sound over the ice. Her boyfriend, Pieter, hunched over a chainsaw, checking its fluids, a can of gasoline beside his knee.

"It's kind of sad," she said, rubbing her arms, "to end this way. Every year. Just to be burned. What was the point of it all?"

They, the neighbors, were approaching now. The first trees being piled in a place far away from shore and the watching houses. A mile away, the city glimmered on a hill. An isthmus city buttressed by two lakes.

Pieter primed the chainsaw's bulb, placed the toe of his boot inside the open handle to steady the saw against the ice, and then jerked the starter cord. The chainsaw rumbled. He raised the saw off the ice and spun its steel teeth; the machine screamed in the night. Kat started. Away from the city even this much, there were no traffic sounds: no buses, no horns, no stereos, no drunk pedestrians. The chainsaw did not seem to belong, and she supposed that thrilled Pieter. There was a wide smile on his face, half hidden beneath his mustache, the corners of which he had waxed into two curls. She did not approve of the mustache and saw the sculpted whiskers there as resembling some kind of ludicrous mantle.

"Oh, it's all good fun," Pieter said, setting the saw down, its small engine still idling. "Besides, it's better than tossing the tree on the curb, isn't it? Something you were supposed to have loved. Just kicked to the curb or dumped into some random ditch. It's like disposing of a body. Naw, this is better.

We get together, build a bonfire, drink some schnapps, maybe some skinny-dipping." He looked at her and grinned.

"You've got to be pulling my leg," she said flatly.

"I wouldn't do that," he said, coming to her, his long fingers in her hair smelling of gasoline and oil, his mustache close to her lips. They kissed and his whiskers tickled her. He had shaved the rest of his beard the night before. A kind of lark. He'd done it while she was sleeping and she woke in the morning beside him, a strange version of her lover, and not for the better.

"It's close to zero," she said. "Also, I'm not sure I like that thing," she said, indicating with her finger his mustache. "Just for the record."

"We also scuba-dive," he said seriously.

"What are you talking about?" she said. "There's not even any open water."

"That's what the chainsaw's for. We make open water," he said. "It's like a dream. A little acid and you'd swear you were on another planet."

"You're not doing that tonight, are you?" she asked, pushing away from him.

"I do it every year. I even brought a wet suit for you. You have to try. No acid tonight. Maybe a little grass. Or just schnapps. Whatever you want."

"I don't fucking believe this," she said, suddenly exhausted. It was not late, though the sun was long gone. Perhaps six in the evening, more people streaming out onto the lake now, four dozen in total. The pyre of desiccated trees growing and the tang of marijuana in the air mixing with the metallic spiciness of schnapps. She watched as a man threw a bucket of kerosene on the pile. Then a young woman hooted and flicked her cigarette butt at the mound. It went twirling through the air, orange and yellow, until it kissed the kerosene and there was a strong huff of a fire starting. The flames climbed quickly. Fifteen, twenty, thirty feet in the air. The crowd roared over the sound of glasses touching. There were many coolers out on that broad plane of ice, and also people simply spilling cases of aluminum cans onto the frozen lake.

"Hey," Pieter said, "hey. You all right? What's going on? Look, you don't have to stay if you don't want to. I'm not forcing you."

She looked away from him to the chainsaw, jostling itself on the ice and putting out a steady blue hiss of smoke. They hadn't been dating long—three months. He was the best lover she'd ever had. Everything that was too much about him in the real world, in the now, was revelatory in her bed. He was wild and uninhibited, strong and creative, stubborn and hypergenerous.

She'd never come before, not until sleeping with him. Their first date, in the days after they met in the amusement park, she had invited him in, something inside her flaring up and against her better judgment. Her fingertips hooked in his belt loops. He pushed her into her bed. Pulled off her boots and blue jeans. With his teeth, yanked off her panties. Then, his eyes on hers, he said, "I'm not going to stop until you come three times." And he put his tongue in her, on her, ate at her like a hummingbird.

He took her face in his hands now and kissed her. "Seriously," he said, "I have to walk back to the house anyway for my wet suit and tanks. I'll take you back."

She surveyed the party. A woman playing an accordion. Some voices caroling, others howling "Hey Jude." The bonfire of Christmas trees so hot no one could stand within thirty feet of it.

"You ever worry about the ice? I mean, does anyone worry about anything?" She wrapped her arms around him. Studied the fire in his eyes.

"The ice has got to be three feet thick by now. Maybe more. Sometimes it's been as much as six. Let's find out. The saw is all warmed up now."

He went to the chainsaw and revved it again, the crowd turning to observe him as he put the spinning blades to the ice. The chainsaw went down easily, spitting chips and splinters of ice, then very cold water at Pieter's calves and thighs. He went slowly, deeply, working the chainsaw in a straight line three feet long. The deeper the blades sunk, the more water surged back at him. His mustache now a frozen shelf over his lip. A minor throng had assembled behind him.

Having finished cutting the square in the ice, he began to cut that plug into smaller pieces. Men came over, carrying lanterns and pulled away the chunks of ice to reveal a portal into the lake, a door of black water. Everyone stared down into it. It was so odd, to hear water lapping in January, to see little black scalloped waves.

"Let's get the equipment and come back," he said. Pieter shut the chainsaw off and reached for Kat's hand. Then he practically ran to the house, dragging her behind, the fire throwing weak shadows in front of them.

Pieter rented the middle floor of a turn-of-the-century Victorian right on the shore. A dump, really. Mice in the drawers and scurrying up and down the pipes, ancient registers pumping out hot steam, the windowpanes coated in complex matrices of frost.

"I think I'll need a drink," she said at last as they entered his apartment. "Or a little weed, maybe? Something to calm me down."

"So you're coming?" he asked, smiling, clearly surprised.

"Sure," she said, feeling some kind of yoke drop away from her shoulders. "What the hell."

"You've scuba-dived before?" he asked, unscrewing a half-empty bottle of red wine and pouring her a full coffee mug.

"Once," she said, "in Mexico. Not like this."

He nodded. "Well, we're going to stay close to one another. It's a lake, not an ocean. So you can't get into too much trouble. And there will also be a cord between us. That's crucial. Don't forget the cord. But inside the suits we'll be plenty warm."

He stared at her as she sipped her wine.

"What?" she asked finally.

"I think we should probably fuck first," he said, pulling off his clothes.

She finished the wine in a gulp, kicked off her mukluks. It was hot enough in the kitchen to break a sweat, a little linoleum-floored sauna. On her knees, she felt granules of salt and sugar bite into her skin, felt her nipples graze the floor before he placed his hands under them. He made her feel unfastened, her body weightless and unencumbered. She was another person while they were intertwined. When they were done, she stood, and outside, the bonfire looked like a raft of angry light.

They held hands as they went back out into the cold in their wet suits, their bodies tightly clad in black, the booties on their feet crunching the snow beneath them. He carried both tanks on his back, the other gear in a bag on his shoulder. Back out on the ice, they had the look of two people with a new secret. Some of Pieter's friends and neighbors hooted at them. He raised a hand in mock triumph; Kat felt herself blush. It was humiliating, this. And thrilling.

Pieter equipped her: tanks, belt, weights, flippers, gloves, a hood. For all the lunacy of this nighttime ice dive, he was scrupulous, his hand flittering all around her, cinching things, scrutinizing gauges and dials, facing her, saying, "How does that feel? You still with me?"

She nodded, thumbs up, watched as he suited himself up, came back to her and said, "We'll go for a half hour. Not long. I've got a rope. I'll tie us together. Keep your hand on the cord if you want to. You can keep us as close together or as far apart as you want. Sometimes it's better to drift a bit. You touch someone in the dark down there, it can give you a little scare. And remember the fire. If something happens, find the fire. The fire is close to our hole. Okay?"

He went first, waddling toward the hole as the crowd applauded, his hands in the air, riling them up, brandishing a huge underwater flashlight in one hand. He fixed his face mask, his snorkel, and then let his body drop through the hole. He was gone.

Suddenly she was unsure. She moved toward the hole. And then his gloved hand appeared out of the water, a few fingers motioning her down. The crowd once again roared. She mimicked his checklist, tightened her face mask and inserted her regulator, took a step and plunged down.

All around her now: darkness; and above, a ceiling of white-blue light, diffused. Just the hole there, the blurry light of a few lanterns and murky movement. She began to hyperventilate, unable to find Pieter, no bottom beneath her, suspended but dropping slowly. She kicked up frantically, only to bump her head on the ice, her hands on it now, searching for an edge that did not exist. She scratched at the ice with her gloved hands. Black creeping in at the sides of her vision. Then: a hand. Pieter.

He was in front of her now, both hands on her shoulders, the flashlight on a cord around his neck. His eyes wide but soft, happy. He took one of her hands and pressed it to his chest. She felt him breathing and it steadied her. Slow. She could feel his ribs and musculature beneath the wet suit. She knew the topography of his body. His heart beating slowly. There had been a shock at first, the water on her cheeks and into the wet suit, but now the shock was gone. It was warmer in the water than outside, above.

They remained that way for a minute or two, paddling their fins, floating, holding on to one another. She watched as the lanterns moved away from the hole and then there was just the flashlight around Pieter's neck, sending a single shaft down into the nothing. She felt better again, her muscles relaxed. She nodded at Pieter and he took the length of rope from off his belt, tying it to her wrist. At maximum, it was fifteen feet long. He pointed and they moved away from the hole, toward a dim light some distance away.

It was the bonfire, she realized, that they were seeing from below. From here, it looked like something in outer space burning, a distant collection of stars, though she knew how wide and tall the fire was up there, on the ice. But directly beneath it, the fire was its own strange aurora, expanding and contrasting, all the colors of the rainbow, roaring silently, the ice under the fire buckling at times and splintering. She was transfixed, wanted to touch it. Did touch the bottom of the ice. A translucent window. A forest of teenage trees, doomed from the start and piled lovingly for this end. She realized that in the spring, when the ice thawed, their skeletons and ashes would sink to the bottom of the lake, a strange aquatic burial.

They moved away from the fire now, away from the light,

the cord attached to her arm growing taut as Pieter disappeared into the unknowable gloom that swallowed him. She followed.

They'd met in the fall, one of the last days of October. A few persistent leaves still clinging to the trees. Kat had agreed to watch her older sister's twelve-year-old, Harrison, for the weekend, though in truth she did not much like children. Her apartment was small, filled with books, and she owned no television. Her nephew was appalled to learn that she did not play video games. They spent Friday night and most of Saturday at the cinema, stealing from one movie theater to the next, taking breaks only to visit the bathroom or buy more popcorn. In the dark they did not have to talk. They watched whatever movies he wanted to see.

But on Sunday she awoke stiff and yearning for fresh air. She roused her nephew and they went out for waffles. Then she drove them south, away from the city, to a giant amusement park. It was the last day of the season and the parking lots were largely abandoned, not a yellow school bus in sight. The tickets were cheap, and they strolled right into the park without waiting, no lines for any of the rides.

She noticed Pieter as they approached the huge roller coaster. He was sitting at the front by himself, a few teenage couples generously spaced behind him. Some of the couples heavy petting, tonguing—no adult supervision at all. Pieter's face was red, as if burned by the wind. He wore a red scarf around his neck, tightly tucked into a winter jacket. His eyes were very dull and red-rimmed, his lips pursed together seriously.

"Aunt Kat," Harrison asked, "can I have a few dollars to play video games? I need a break from these rides." He stuck out his hand.

"Just call me Kat, please," she said, giving the boy two dollars. He looked at her and then at the two dollars and then back at her. She realized two dollars would not last him long and gave him two more. The weekend had grown expensive. She watched the boy duck into a nearby arcade, also abandoned, the screens of a few video games flashing.

She watched Pieter ride the roller coaster repeatedly, the other riders disembarking each time while he remained motionless at the front of the car. She sat on a park bench, the day gray, a cold wind rearranging her curly brown hair, her cheeks pink. After a scant ten minutes, Harrison returned from the arcade and sat down close beside her. The roller coaster came to yet another stop and a few riders drifted off, giving each other high fives. Again Pieter persisted, just wiped his nose solemnly with a Kleenex. Harrison looked at her.

"You want to ride that one?" he asked.

"Yeah," she said at last, "why not?"

They ran to the snake of seats before the metal bars came down. Two protective harnesses swung down from above and rested snugly over and across their chests, Harrison looking small behind his. It was just the three of them. Kat and

Harrison nine rows behind Pieter. The ride jerked forward, began to rise up its steep steel slope.

At the top of the incline, the park spread out beneath them, her Subaru visible far away in the white crosshatched parking lot. And then the rush forward. Kat watched as Pieter disappeared down and away and felt her stomach lurch forward as the cars gained speed and the world slipped out from underneath them. She screamed and clutched the steel brace pressed to her chest. The rushing wind cut her face as they tore through the route of the coaster, metal on metal impossibly loud and her head jarring constantly so her perception of the world was as though she were watching a bad home recording, images jerking and bouncing. She stopped screaming and focused on breathing. Beside her, Harrison was cheering. The ride spun, as if a corkscrew shot from some giant cannon, and they twisted upside down repeatedly, Kat's hair in her face, spare change dropping out of her blue jeans and plunking loudly against the steel car.

And then the ride slowed and came to a stop at the same platform where they had boarded.

"That was amazing!" Harrison said.

The harnesses all lifted in a hiss of hydraulics and they were free to depart, but she could see that the lone rider up ahead remained where he was.

"Want to ride again?" Kat asked.

Harrison smiled, punched her lightly in the arm. "You're kidding me, right? You were, like, dying back there!" He laughed.

"Well, anyway," she said, ignoring him, "I'm staying."

"Seriously? All right! All right! All right! Awesome!"

The harnesses dropped back down into place and they rocked forward. She was focused on Pieter's head, his rigid shoulders, the hands she could not see, but knew must be resting in his lap, as if he were at church. The roller coaster began its climb, then rattled down and around its course, Harrison giggling and screaming, his voice high-pitched as a girl's. Kat's eyes remained trained on the back of Pieter's head. He never moved.

It wasn't as bad the second time around—the loop-de-loops, the hairpin turns, the three-g drops. And it wasn't long before the roller coaster returned to its station; Pieter un-moving.

"Come on," Kat said to Harrison, "we're moving up to the front, where it's scarier."

"Awesome," he agreed.

As they installed themselves immediately behind Pieter, Kat leaned forward before the braces came down and said into his ear, "You all right up there? You haven't moved in a half hour."

He started, which had the effect of startling her too, and turned to look at her. He was very handsome, the bones of his face well-defined. There were tears on his face.

"Oh, you're crying," Kat said. "I'm sorry."

"It's okay," he said. "It's just the cold. I can't help it." And then "I'm also a little high."

The harnesses came down again and they were off, racing through the pale slate sky, their voices alternating between shrieks, obscenities, and laughter. The world began to slow as they became accustomed to the reckless speed of the ride. Kat watched the landscape below: janitors chasing blowing garbage, vendors eating clouds of cotton candy, security guards smoking cigarettes. She watched Pieter's head: his thick hair, the corded muscles of his neck, his perfectly shaped ears, like the shells of some beautiful species of snail.

Finally Pieter rose from the ride, his legs for the briefest of moments wobbly. She watched him go toward a bathroom, where he disappeared. Harrison, beside her, almost uncontrollable with glee.

"I heard you say *fuck*!" he said, punching her stomach and laughing. "You're the best aunt ever!"

She watched the restroom pavilion, its door marked MEN. Her heart, suddenly light, lost, unbound—how?

"What?" Harrison asked. "Think he's gonna puke or something?"

"Let's go see," she said. They walked toward the restrooms, sitting on a bench, Harrison's body beside her, electric with excitement and trembling with the cold. She felt his yet-boy body beside hers.

Pieter came out of the restroom, wiping his lips and forehead with a sheet of brown paper toweling. Kat stood from the bench but did not approach him. Suddenly her voice would not work and she could not recall her own bravery on the roller coaster, her ability there to speak to this beautiful man.

"So, did you ralph in there or what?" Harrison asked.

Pieter looked at them and smiled easily. As he approached them, she fell in love with his walk too. He seemed to move side to side even as he strutted forward, his knees more like leather hinges than bone, his narrow hips swaying, stomach flat as a barn board, beneath a wider, flat chest. He moved casually toward them, as if wading through a Floridian pool, gin and tonic in hand.

Pieter looked at her and then down at Harrison, "All over the place," he said after several beats. "Go check it out. But don't slip."

Harrison ran off.

Pieter extended his long hand and said, "Pieter."

"Kat."

"I want your telephone number, please," he said.

She reached into her purse, fumbling, struggling for a pen, a pencil, chalk, anything. Finally she found a pen, but the ink was gone, dried up. She threw it to the ground and continued searching. He knelt down for the pen, removed its cap, stuck the tip of the pen to his tongue, and said, "Never mind. Here's mine." And then he took her hand, lifted her sleeve up, and began to write. Seven numbers in blue ink. He pressed hard enough that she worried, then hoped, the numerals would be like a tattoo. She studied the number.

"Now yours," he said, holding the pen over his own naked forearm. She told him.

Harrison came running out of the restroom. "You must've had mushrooms for breakfast."

Pieter smiled. "Bingo." And then he waved and ambled away.

They moved through the cold darkness together, so close that though Kat could not see Pieter, she could feel his rubber-suited body, his flippers moving the cold black water. Here the world was a featureless vacuum, her body weightless, only the faint sounds of her own respiration and the tiny feel of bubbles brushing against her face and goggles. She simply moved forward, unencumbered, toward what she assumed were the vague lights of the city above: the distant lights of restaurants where she dined, bars where she drank, her own dull office, the state capitol's tall dome—her familiar world.

Reaching for the cord knotted to her arm, she jerked it slightly, then stopped and hung in the water, kicking her feet placidly, aware of her own lungs. Pieter came to her, his light turning slowly. He aimed the beam below her and for some time they were like that, facing each other, their hands cradling each other's elbows above the quiet pumping of their legs. They stared at each other; seconds drawn out into epochs, time crystallizing like molecules of water becoming ice. Then he let go and she followed him, back the way they had come, she supposed. Though she did not know.

She did not notice at first the absence of his light. Only after kicking for what felt like several yards did she stop and begin ever so slowly sinking. She looked ahead but did not see. Did not see Pieter or the single ray of his flashlight.

And then, as her senses expanded and fear began to reach up from the bottom of the cold, black winter lake, she reached for the cord and felt nothing about her arm. Panicking, she touched one arm and then the other, swept at her arms as if they were covered in spiders, centipedes. She forgot to breathe and kicked up until she felt the lid of the lake against her scalp—the top of her own icy coffin—and began pounding futilely, the very bones in her fingers close to breaking.

Pieter had come home from Afghanistan, and nineteen days later his parents announced their divorce. He told Kat about the day he'd spent packing a U-Haul truck from the first bluing of dawn to the fading purple of dusk. His mother hadn't packed anything, so he'd had to do most of the work for her. Everything into cardboard boxes she had taken from behind a liquor store. Her knickknacks. Her sewing materials. Her collections of miniature silver spoons, odd-shaped mirrors, teddy bears. Her linens and clothing, her romance novels, her drawers of unlighted candles, her grandmother's china, old photo albums. Everything—her life. He wrapped it all in newspaper and walked it out to the U-Haul. She supervised the landing of every box, the placement of each piece of furniture.

Pieter's father had gone to the family's cabin in Door County, a peninsular thumb out into Lake Michigan.

Pieter's mother told him in summation, "We had just

enough energy to see our marriage through until your return. We needed each other just enough to see you step off that plane. We couldn't have gone through it alone or separate. And my new guy, Dennis, he doesn't understand. Not really. But I can't be with your father anymore. The best thing we ever did, the best thing *I* ever did—was you."

Pieter drove the U-Haul to a storage unit beside the highway and unloaded the truck, the headlights of the rented vehicle shining into the empty cave of space.

He slept many hours a day in his childhood bedroom, the blinds drawn, the bedroom dark. He had no nightmares. He rose only to visit the bathroom, eat a bowl of cereal, sometimes to watch ESPN for hours at a time, trying to detect minute differences in the *SportsCenter* program that repeated itself almost constantly from six in the morning until noon—the only thing he cared to look at. Young men, men his age, men like those he had befriended in Afghanistan. Athletic, sweating, running, screaming, attacking one another, knocking one another down. He would mute the television and watch helmet-to-helmet tackles, fierce cross-checks into glass and boards, home-plate collisions, tomahawk dunks. And he felt that.

Also, drugs. When his father returned, they drank together. United against the day-dark winter and the enshrouding blizzards. In spring, delighting in the melt off the gutters, in the push of daffodils and tulips, the greening of the grass. In summer they did not combat the humidity;

kept the air conditioner off. What money his father figured he saved from conserved energy went into canned beer, cold and light and golden.

Pieter said to Kat one evening in bed, "You know how to maximize efficiency in a refrigerator?"

She turned to look at him and she was laughing softly, her hand on his shoulder. "No," she said, feigning seriousness.

"You fill it with cans of beer. Bottles of beer. All that thermal mass. Glass or aluminum. Doesn't matter. Beer. The machine doesn't have to work so hard to cool something. The cold stays right in the liquid. In the containers themselves."

And so father and son drank themselves right through autumn, mourning the dimmed-down sun and the burned-out leaves. Pieter introduced his dad to marijuana. They sat in the backyard and passed a little pipe.

That summer he visited the amusement park with a friend from high school, another marine who had served in Iraq. They'd begun spending time together, throwing horseshoes at the VFW or driving the backroads, flinging empties into the ditches. They didn't talk much to each other, too much time between them to bother filling, and it was okay because it was enough simply not to be alone. This friend Duane *did* have dreams, nightmares. Screamers, sheet-soakers, ghosts in his skull. The police had come to Duane's apartment four different times, and always in the middle of the night. The first three times they kicked in the door. By the fourth, Duane was leaving it unlocked. The neighbors had called 9-1-1; it sounded like a murder in progress.

They went to the amusement park because there was no entrance fee for veterans and because a therapist had told Duane that it was as good a place as any to *feel something* without filling his veins or nostrils or lungs. So they went four times a week, as if it were a job, arriving early and staying late. Sometimes they picked up a couple of girls and later they'd follow them back to a dormitory, a motel, a town house. They ate junk food: elephant ears and powdered sugar, corn dogs, soda, fried candy bars. They wore uniforms: sneakers, shorts, muscle shirts to show off their biceps and military tattoos, their shrapnel scars and the brands of super-hot cigarette lighters; the black moons of stubbed-out cigarette butts and the places on their bodies they pointed to drunk and told each other, "Titus grabbed my forearm right here. His hand was right here. His grip was so fucking strong that I thought he was going to break my arm in half."

But despite Duane's therapist's best intentions, they rarely felt anything at all. Just an oddly intense desire to return to the action they'd once so detested.

"So, why did you keep going?" Kat asked him. "Why were you there that day?"

"I don't know," Pieter said. "You have to try . . . You know? You want to feel something. Is it okay if we don't talk about it?" Then: "I feel something now. Here." And he had placed his hand firmly, warmly, on her mons pubis and turned to her and said, "Is it okay if we fuck again?"

She didn't recognize it in the first few weeks as addiction. He was just incandescent, inexhaustible. They had sex, fucked, made love, before dinner and after. He woke her in the middle of the night, his head buried between her legs. And now that sex was enjoyable—a revelation—her body no longer muted or a disappointment but rather its own set of fireworks, she always acquiesced, always. They grew skinnier together, burning each other down, feeding each other nothing but motion and sweat.

They had their own places and she had her job, working as a graphic designer for the state's lottery. She sketched and colored the one-dollar scratch-offs found in every gas station from Beloit to Bloomer. Calling him, ringing the ancient telephone in his apartment at the end of her day, the promise of his body—all this made her days easier. And there were no commitments. Some weekends he was gone—to be with his father, to clean the cabin, to visit his mother and her new fiancé.

But she loved him. Did not yet *know* all of him or understand all of him, but she wanted to. She had not yet known him all of one season and wondered if they would always have the energy to expend on each other that they had then—their bodies young, everything still fresh and curious.

He had bought her a dildo for the times when he was away, and she would lay in her bed alone while he was gone, staring out the window of her apartment at the lights of the city and the flat white plain of the lake, but the purple toy only made her more lonely for him. She kept it inside a cotton bag in a drawer, the drawstring neatly bowtied.

She worried that she would get tired. She worried about so many things. She did not know how not to worry. In bed, without Pieter, she would think about work or her car and how it needed an oil change, a new windshield, more pressure in the balding tires. She would think about her sister, about how she ought to call her more. She would think about visiting her aging parents up in Cadott. About how she ought to exercise more. Why didn't she use the time she spent worrying to exercise more? Why didn't she leave her bed and lay on the floor, crunching her stomach muscles into Jillian Michaels's flatness? Why didn't she go back to school, graduate school? How many nights had she started applications before simply abandoning the process to gorge on hours of Netflix or Hulu? Hours and hours becoming whole days she'd never ever recover, totally wasted on television she'd already watched a whole decade before.

In the past, it had begun to interrupt and then dissolve her relationships with men. She worried about calling them or their not calling her. Sometimes in the nights, frequently on the cusp of too late, she did call them, her voice perhaps a little too earnest, the desperation in it a little too honeyed. It had shocked her that such a gesture, a friendly telephone call, could be enough to tip things into silence or anonymity. And then they disappeared from her world: her Facebook, her email, their telephone numbers changed, disconnected.

And then, undone and alone again, she tried to put the worry away. She would go out on a Friday night with a friend and drink too fast. Approach a man at a bar, even an ugly one, and try to take him home or get his number. But those nights were failures as well, her tack always too eager, too forceful, her face too shining, her eyes too clear or too sad. Something.

But with Pieter she felt swaddled. Swallowed by his strength. He would not let her get away or come unraveled. Even this, though, his gravity, worried her.

She worried about the near-invisible dimpling on her thighs. She worried about her student loans: $52,161.00. She worried about the shape and length of her pubic hair. She worried about her mother's increasing forgetfulness. She worried about the whiteness of her teeth. She worried about her inability to finish *Moby-Dick*. She worried about Pieter. She worried about love.

Just then and through the blackness, a light: bright white and cold and enough to make her heart stop its wild pounding. Pieter. He grabbed her arms and held her away from his body. But she would not look at him. He wrapped himself around her, held her face in place and stared at her. She sealed her eyes against him, against this underwater nightmare he'd dragged her into. When she opened them he held the cord, in his hands, pulled it, and her arm jerked gently, like a marionette. His eyes were calm. She could see that, the light told her that. He took her gloved hand and led them purposefully. In the distance she sensed a warm glow and a hint of movement. *The bonfire,* she thought. Her mind was foggy. *What were those other movements?* Freshwater dolphins? No. Great fishes? Seals? Her hands hurt and there was barely spirit enough inside her to move the flippers and propel herself through the water. She felt dragged along, the way she imagined a net followed a boat, the rope between them taut. They were moving quickly toward the light now, and she could see bodies in motion, the crash of divers plunging down, naked, their flesh very pale and some of the women not entirely nude, but wearing brightly colored lingerie. The thrashing of bare feet and sudden sweeping of hands unnerved her after so much time in such austere silence, stillness. Here, underneath the bonfire, the water felt warmer. *Could that be?* she thought.

And then, *Why did he leave me?*

Pushing through the school of swimmers Pieter rocketed out of the water. A moment later, his two black-gloved hands plunged down and she took them.

On the ice he tore off her mask and she gasped in the cold air for several moments. A blanket came for her shoulders and he began stripping off the gear that all of a sudden felt impossibly heavy. He lifted her blanketed body up, carried her toward the bonfire, now substantially diminished, and though he laid her down some twenty feet away, she still felt as if she were bathing in the oppressive heat of a blast furnace. She stared at the fire. He touched her all over, rubbed her shoulders, ran his fingers on her face, held her head to his chest. His mustache had drooped over his lip, obscured his teeth.

"Why did you leave me?" she asked finally.

"What?" he said.

She began to cry. "You *left* me. Down there. In the fucking dark."

"No," he said, "we were always together. We were always tied together. Always."

"No we *weren't!*" she screamed. "No we weren't!"

They were aware of faces turning toward them, toward the fire.

"Kat," he said calmly, "Kat. I would never do that to anyone. Never."

But she would not look at him. There were many bottles littered upon the ice, and cans. In the air, the tang of marijuana and the smell of pine comingled.

"Kat," he repeated.

"What?"

"Kat," he said. "Kat, please."

She looked at her arm, where the cord was still tied about her thin wrist. It lay on the ice between them, already frozen in the unrelenting cold, and the stars above them blinking and throbbing. The bonfire popped and wheezed, and she watched as many millions of balsam and fir needles went white with heat before incinerating into nothing.

"Kat," he said, "look at me."

But she stood and walked away from the bonfire, toward

the sleeping neighborhood where her little blue car was parked, while behind her, skinny-dippers were still laughing and someone had started the chainsaw again to cut another hole. She walked away, the wet suit a second, thickened skin, and she did not know what or how to feel anymore. Behind her, the frozen cord dragged from her wrist and Pieter stood still, calling her name out over the frozen lake.

SWEET LIGHT CRUDE

PRELUDE

"The day of the spill," Foreman said into the pay phone, "I was out in my rowboat. Right out there on that little lake. I call it my pond. The lake is so small a person hardly needs a motor, but the fact is, I'm getting old, weak. So last summer I attached a little two-horse Evinrude. Bought it at an estate sale for five dollars. Thing gets me across the lake in half a minute. Saves my back and arms.

"Anyhow, I was out that day, fishing. Nothing biting. So I used the motor a lot. Back and forth, figuring if they weren't biting in one corner of the pond, they'd be biting in another. Maybe if I ran that little motor enough I could herd 'em all into one little bay and clobber 'em. Slay bluegills and crappie all day and have myself a little dinner.

"It got to be about lunchtime and I went in. My bladder

isn't what it used to be, either. Was a time I could piss into a coffee can I kept for bailing and just fling the output into the lake, but now I ain't agile or dexterous enough. Afraid I'd flip the boat. So I went in. Turned on the radio. That's when I heard.

"The man on the radio talked about flames hundreds of feet high. Clouds of black smoke. People dead in the water, blown to smithereens. No end in sight, either, just oil gushing out of the ocean floor. I heard people days later down at the café in town, and they said it was like the planet was bleeding. I suppose that's about right."

The old man dropped two dollars' worth of quarters into the pay phone and scanned the road for passing vehicles. Nothing. Just him alone in this rest area of picnic benches and lichen-encrusted boulders. The badly potholed parking lot in need of new yellow paint. A historical marker recalling French voyageurs and canoes full of fur, beads, blankets, knives.

"Day of the spill I came back out of the cabin and walked down to the pond. I was just about back in the boat when I looked at my pond. There was oil in the water. Not much. You know how it is, though. You got to mix your gasoline with oil for them two-stroke motors and there must have been some kind of leak in my line. And I could see right there in the water where I'd been. Like tracks you see, trails of oil. Them rainbows, everywhere. God, I felt so bad."

The old man was quiet a moment, then wondered if he

even still had the connection. Could not even hear his contact breathing, coughing, anything.

"You still there?" he said, hoarse.

"I'm here. I'm listening to everything."

"Good, that's good. I don't mean to ramble on, such as I am. But I'm alone now, and goddamnit, I want to help. To be of assistance. Well, I seen that pond all coated in oil and I took the motor right off and threw it in the shed. I was so embarrassed. I can't tell you. I ain't been fishing since. I swear.

"Anyhow, I don't have much time," the old man said into the receiver, "and I don't have nothin' to lose. So I'm willing to help out. Any way I can. You tell me what you want me to do and I'll do it."

HOUR FOUR

Hazelwood's lips were black from the oil, and there was oil on the old floorboards from where he had already spilled three glassfuls. Foreman refilled the juice glass from a five-gallon plastic jug full of sweet light crude that sat beside the only door of the little cabin. It went into the clear vessel and might have been prune juice, though there was the smell, the strange rainbow sheen of its surface. The old table was now ruined, slicked over with oil. The table was older than the cabin, built by Foreman's immigrant kin long gone. The room was cold. It was autumn on the northern tier, the rusted leaves of fall already down in a dry carpeting. The sky outside gray.

Foreman set the glass down again in the middle of the table and fed the small fire in the hearth with kindling. Just enough heat to warm his palms and his kneecaps when he bent close to the little flames. Hazelwood remained at the table, three of his limbs duct-taped to the wooden chair, one hand free as could be.

"Can I have a cigarette?" Hazelwood asked.

Foreman shrugged, reached into his breast pocket for the pack, shook one cigarette loose, and placed it between the man's oily lips, the oil already drying there, crusting. He lit a match and held it before the man's face. Hazelwood leaned into the flame and inhaled. The cashmere sweater he wore, once white, now was spangled in black and muddy at the elbows. His khakis too, stained and ruined. His loafers ridiculous for the country around him. The combed lines of his thick head of aristocratic silver hair had somehow endured despite the impact of the sawed-off baseball bat Foreman thumped him with. Hazelwood's eyes very blue and hard.

With his one free hand Hazelwood removed the cigarette and said, "I could drop this cigarette to that spill there, start a fire."

"Go on," said Foreman, "save me the trouble. I'm giving you a chance." Then "You don't know shit about fire. I could spit such a fire as that out. Piss it out if I had to. What you need is gasoline. Jet fuel. Kerosene. If you want a fire.

If I was you I'd stop spilling that shit and get it over with. But you assholes, you like to spill. Don't you?"

Hazelwood inhaled again, blew a stream of smoke at Foreman. His smile was black, a thin veneer of oil on his otherwise perfectly white and aligned teeth.

"I know fire," Hazelwood said. "You don't become CEO of one of the world's largest oil corporations without knowing about fire. Every Detroit engine is based on fire. Every home furnace. Don't condescend to me."

Foreman walked over to the man and punched him in the kidney as if he were a side of beef. Hazelwood coughed, spitting blood and oil comingled.

After a time he looked at Foreman. "Where'd you even get that stuff?" he asked, pointing to the jerry can. "Not like it's available on the open market. Normal people can't just buy that."

Foreman pulled a chair toward the hearth, began whittling a little branch of dogwood into a point.

"It wasn't so hard," he said, not looking at Hazelwood. "Turns out there's a damn ocean of the shit down off Florida. Off Louisiana. Off Alabama and Mississippi. I don't know if you seen that on the news or not. A fucking well blew up. Millions of gallons everywhere. A friend sent it to me. Loaded it on the back end of an eighteen-wheeler along with the last shipment of oysters and shrimp bound for Minneapolis. Trucker brought it up here for free. As a favor. Once he heard what our plan was for you."

"*Our* plan?"

"Never mind."

"Huh. It's all bigger than me, you know," Hazelwood said. "People think these things, these drills and spills and tankers and pipelines. They think they're one thing. They think you can just put your finger on that one thing and call it bad, but it doesn't work like that. Half the time companies send out a press release, they're doing it to rile up stockholders, future stock buyers. They'll build a road to a future mine site just to generate excitement. We drill for oil somewhere, we don't even always intend to get that oil out right away. See what I mean? How big it is? I didn't spill that oil down there. There are about three companies between me and that responsibility. Three boards, three CEOs, three companies worth billions in stock. You understand? I'm not the bad guy."

Foreman rose and moved away from the fire to the other end of the table. He watched Hazelwood smoke, suddenly very tired. A draft blew through the cabin and shook the windowpanes.

"This place yours?" Hazelwood asked.

"I ain't here for a dialogue," said Foreman. "This here is about penance." He smiled coolly, folded his hands on the table, considered his fingernails and the sliver moons of dirt and oil beneath them. He saw that Hazelwood was not afraid. He wondered if the man's wealth was some kind of comfort to him. "You knew that well would fail."

"No, I did not."

"You knew that it probably would, and you didn't do anything about it."

"Not my company."

"It was your oil."

"It was their failure. Their systemic failure. My company has a nearly unblemished environmental track record. Look, we sponsor whale research in the Antarctic Ocean, rhino research in southern Africa. We fund some guy around these parts who's obsessed with dragonflies."

"Oh, bullshit. You pricks are corrupt as the day is long, and you know it. Greedy is what you are." Foreman pounded the table and the juice glass of oil trembled, the black liquid sloshing to its rim.

"How much is it you want me to know, anyway? I mean, how much can I really be responsible for?"

"Everything. It's your company. You get the big bonuses. You cash those checks, don't you? The big tax breaks. Why are you immune from the big penalties?"

"And this is a penalty?"

Foreman inhaled the last vapors of Hazelwood's cigarette intermingled with the smell of the woodsmoke and the cold. "Recompense. Justice. Just deserts. I don't know anymore. Something. Something." Foreman pushed the glass toward Hazelwood. "Drink up and I'll take you to a hospital."

"It'll kill me."

"Maybe. Maybe not. I promise you this: I'll get you to that hospital quick as I can. Thirty-minute ride. If you can't talk, I'll talk for you. I'll own up to what I've done to you."

"I don't believe you."

"Or I can set fire to this cabin with you in it and they won't find you at all."

Hazelwood fidgeted against the chair, but he was bound tight. "I'm done with this cigarette."

"Drop it away from that spilled oil."

Hazelwood did so and Foreman rose to collect the smoldering butt, tossing it into the fireplace. His back to Hazelwood, he heard the glass once again knocked off the table, the vessel finally breaking, oil joining oil in a black puddle on the floor.

Hazelwood laughed. "You dumb old fuck," he said. "We can do this all day."

Foreman turned to observe the viscous spill on the floorboards. He watched the fluid find the irregularities of the floor, the rises and falls. After several moments the oil pooled in one place and was still. Foreman said nothing. He did not have much time, but he had time enough. He looked at the CEO.

Foreman said, "I got the cancer."

"The fuck do I care? You fucking kidnapped me."

"You should care. I just told you all you need to know."

Foreman kneeled beside the fire, probed the embers of the little fire with a poker. His hands were gnarled, the nails flat and yellowed. Along his forearm and wrists the sign of needles marking the course of his blue veins—where the treatments had been plumbed into him. His arm hair was white over a tanned brown flesh peppered by liver spots. He would leave behind no widow and no orphans. There was just enough left inside him for one more thing, and then that was it.

"What I know now is that you're the one in need of a hospital. More than me. I can wait you out."

"Ain't nothing they can do for me anymore," Foreman said. He coughed. "They laid out my options before me, and the only thing left is more chemo. I done the chemo for three years. My wife died. I was too weak to come to her funeral. Puking in a goddamned bed skinny as a scarecrow. We were married forty-four years."

Hazelwood looked irritated, puzzled. "Why are you telling me all this?"

"You're a dumb sumbitch, ain't you?" Foreman said, and it gave him some level of pleasure to talk to a powerful man with such indignity.

"They'll find me. You know they will. Everyone's looking. Won't be long. Won't be long and we'll be surrounded. You know how this ends."

Foreman nodded, smiled, "Here's how it goes. You don't get shit 'til you drink that crude. You don't get water. You don't get bread. You don't get to take a piss. You just sit there and look. You decide. How long can you go? It's up to you. Will they find us before that time? Will some goddamned jarhead sniper pick me off? I don't know. But we're well hid. I got what I need. An icebox well stocked. Water, beer, cheese, bread, butter, apples, lemons, fish, steak, mushrooms, onions, eggs. I brought books. Poems. I have started to read poems, you know, since I began my dying. So, Mr. Hazelwood, I really don't give a shit. I'll just sit by the fire and read. And I got a hunch that we're hid better here than you think. We're a four-day hide. Maybe five. What I mean is, even with them searching twenty-four and seven, I still think it'll take 'em that long to come knocking on yonder door. Question you got to ask yourself is, Can you make it five days? Four days? Three days? Two days?"

Hazelwood spat at Foreman's boots.

"If I were you," Foreman said, "I'd save my water. You dumb prick." He stoked the fire, and on his grizzled face the light was a dirty gold and he allowed himself to smile, his old teeth almost worn down. It was the gloaming, evening already settling onto the shoulders of the land.

HOUR EIGHT

"How did you find me?"

Foreman rocked a chair, smoked a filterless cigarette, the paper dry on his lips. The fireplace popped and sucked air. Through the trees, the sound of a wolf. Foreman leaned forward in his chair and listened to the animal's call and it was everything he might have sung too.

"How did you find me?"

The oil in a new tin cup, on the table before Hazelwood.

Foreman coughed, his body riddled with pains everywhere. His bones a matrix of agony. "Soon as that well blew up, a call went out. No, that ain't right. It was after that dumb-ass press conference of yours. Right after that. Then we all saw you again, racing yachts and what have you. Oil spewing out into the ocean and you're racing yachts, as if you lived on another planet entire."

"A call?"

"I guess they call it ecoterrorism now. Back then, we were just burning down signs, blowing dams, spiking trees. Anyway, there's a few of us left. We slipped back into things, the world. There wasn't a name back then for what we were doing, but we're all still out here. Free. No trace of what we done or who we were. But we're still connected to one another, you know. You see a computer around here? We use the mail. Pay telephones. Word of mouth. I was a monkey wrencher from way back. Then I got married. Got straight, laid low. Didn't harm no one. But now I'm going to do this one last thing. You." Foreman pointed a finger at Hazelwood.

"Who called you?"

"Oh, no, I don't think so."

"What does it matter? I'm probably going to die here anyway. That's your grand plan, isn't it? I die if I drink the oil, and I die if I don't drink the oil. Sort of a win-win for the insane, aged ecoterrorists."

Foreman looked out the window. He studied the needles of a nearby white pine outside, its trunk nearly four feet wide at the base. An old thing left over from another time. A historical marker. "A buddy," he said, exhaling. "His brother's a shrimper down there. Got a sick kid with sky-high medical bills. Hard to pay bills when all the shrimp tastes like Castrol."

"But how . . . how did . . . How'd anyone know I'd be up here?"

"Just because we don't have the Internet doesn't mean none of us don't use the Internet. There are libraries. Cafés. Friends. They watched you. That fucking yacht race or what have you. Real sensitive. Then the backlash and you disappeared. Someone found your biography. Guessed you might come home. We found out about your cabin. If that's what you call it. Goddamn castle. I was embarrassed at first. Couldn't believe an ingrate such as yourself could've come out of here."

"I left this place as soon as I could."

"Yeah? Should've stayed gone."

"Should have."

Hazelwood spat on the floor again. "I'm thirsty," he said.

Foreman raised an eyebrow and after a few moments rose from his chair and went to the old refrigerator, which ran off a generator behind the cabin, both machines humming and rumbling more or less incessantly. He extracted a tall pitcher of water and shut the refrigerator's ancient and heavy door. Reached into a cabinet and produced a small glass, then sat back down opposite Hazelwood and placed the pitcher of water on the table. He held up the glass.

"When they first found the tumor," Foreman said, "they cut it out of me. Put me on all kinds of pills. Had me taking vitamins. This glass here was my best friend. Wake up in the morning and eat breakfast, make coffee, write a letter. Then sit down and eat my vitamins. Put one in my mouth and drink a glass of water. Put another in my mouth and drink a glass of water. And so on." He filled it with water. "This is my pill glass."

Hazelwood licked his chapped lips.

"This is artesian water. Come up out of the ground in a secret place not five hundred yards from here. Bubbling forth. It tastes sweet to me. Untainted. Days I'd be out hunting or come back from a fishing trip and I'd walk that path out there to the spring and get down on all fours and drink right out of the earth. Sometimes I'd scare deer or bear doing the same thing. Cold too. Goddamn, is it cold there. Cold and sweet." Foreman held the glass in a toast to Hazelwood. "Mud in your eye."

He drank it all down in two gulps and poured another. He drank and drank. He drank until his guts were cool and overfull. He let some of the water run down the crease of his old chin and intermingle with his whiskers. He stared at Hazelwood and said, "I'm going to take a piss now, and then I'm coming back in here, and when I do I'm going to make a steak. I'm going to sauté some mushrooms and onions and I'm going to pour myself a glass of wine." He stood up, turned to Hazelwood. "Thing is, as sick as I am, I don't get hungry much anymore. But it'll give me some pleasure to eat in front of you."

He left the table and walked outside. He undid his belt and the zipper of his pants and urinated. The night was crisp and he shuddered. The ground smoked where he pissed. His pants were too loose and he cinched the ancient belt over his bony hips; a series of new hand-tooled holes in the belt, bored there with his pocketknife. A rush of loneliness swept over him and he recalled his wife, the nights and days they had spent in the cabin, the sound of her feet on the floorboards. Then the loneliness was replaced with something like determination, because the only thing left for him was the notion that she was waiting for him beyond, beckoning to him like a star or a ball of light both warm and cool all at once, distant and so familiar. He did not believe in God, but he believed in her out there somewhere, and he had to, else the world was too bleak for him to continue. He went back into the cabin.

The tin cup was on the floor in another pond of oil, the floor stained anew. Hazelwood's chair was tipped over, his free arm pinned beneath him, one foot in the air, flailing. Both loafers off and his feet white blue with cold. Foreman lifted the man and the chair back upright; he felt strong when it came to punishing the younger man.

Suddenly Hazelwood swung at him with his free hand but Foreman deflected it and punched the CEO in his teeth. Hazelwood cried out, tears in his eyes, and for the first time he looked scared. Hazelwood spat a bloody tooth into the spilled oil. Then he regained his composure, hissed through a hole in his smile, "I'm going to fucking kill you."

"You're wasting time," Foreman said evenly and moved toward the stove, where he positioned an iron skillet onto an old propane burner. From the refrigerator he removed a piece of red meat. He set it on a white plate. Proceeded to season the steak with salt, pepper, garlic. In the pan he dropped a pat of butter. He chopped onions, garlic, mushrooms. Added them to the pan, reduced the heat. He peered at the flame below the pan and reduced the fire to a minor candle.

"I always cook things out of order," he said. "Greta never would've started them onions and mushrooms so quickly."

Foreman found another pan and set it on the stove over a separate burner. "I prefer to grill," he explained, "but the situation, such as it is." He shrugged. From the pantry: a bottle of red wine. He found another glass.

"I'll let you cut that oil," Foreman offered. "If that'd help. Pour it all into one big mug."

"Fuck you," said Hazelwood.

"I met a man once. A vintner from Argentina. You know what he told me? He told me wine cellars are for the vain. He told me, don't ever keep more than six bottles of wine in your house. Keep what you can drink. What your friends can drink. Think about a party. Keep that much wine. You know why? This vintner, this old man, he told me, you keep a cellar, so what? Someday you're going to die with all those bottles in some dark room and you'll never even have tasted them. And they're down there for what? So one of your kids can drink them? So they get to auction your collection like a bunch of goddamned stamps? No. Drink your wine. Always be drinking wine. That's what he told me. Man was a millionaire many times over and he didn't have a wine cellar. He owned two or three vineyards, but inside his own estate, he never kept no more than a case of wine.

"Day after I first spotted you, I bought this. It's French. You imagine? A bottle all the way from France somehow found its way up here. Nowhere. Another thing: that old vintner. When I met him, he was ninety-one years old. Married to a forty-year-old woman who looked like Sophia Loren."

He laid the meat into the skillet with some butter and minced garlic and, leaning forward, wafted the cooking smells up into his nose.

"You are one sick old bastard," Hazelwood said.

"The thing is, I can't hardly taste anymore. Something about the cancer. Stole my taste right out of me. But I'll tell you what, I *can* taste garlic. I can still *taste* garlic." Foreman flipped the steak with a long-tined fork. "I like it rare. Juicy. I like to taste the animal." He examined the other pan: the onions caramelizing, the mushrooms fragrant. He waited another moment or two, lifted the steak onto the plate, then spooned the mushrooms and onions beside it. He brought the plate to the table and his glass of wine also.

"Shit," Foreman said. "How rude of me." He stood from the table and reached for the tin cup on the floor of the cabin. He went to the door where the jug of oil sat. He refilled the cup and set it before Hazelwood. Then he returned to his place. Raised his glass again.

"To greed," Foreman said. "You're greedy for money and oil. And I'm greedy for this here free-range steak and glass of wine."

He drank. "Oh," he said, "this is good. I can't taste much anymore, but I can taste this. You know what's striking? The mouthfeel. It's both thick and juicy in my mouth. But there's some acid too. Something cleaning up my palate."

He began to saw into the pink of the steak. "You strike me as a man with a wine cellar," he said, his mouth full.

"I have four," Hazelwood said. "My wife and I own a vineyard in California."

"Well," said Foreman, wiping his mouth with a handkerchief, "I guess that's too bad."

HOUR TEN

Hazelwood was squirming in his chair, Foreman sitting heavily in his own. The plate empty and streaked with thin blood, his wineglass again full and the bottle thoroughly diminished. Foreman picked at his teeth, now purple with wine.

"I'm about to piss myself," said Hazelwood.

Foreman shrugged.

Below the confined man, a new stain began to spread, acrid and yellow. The man's khaki pants wet at the crotch and all down his legs to his numb, blue feet. Hazelwood stared at Foreman.

"Jesus, can I get a blanket or something? I'd like a motherfucking blanket at least. Something to cover my feet for the night."

Foreman nodded. "Yeah, it is about that time."

He rose from the table and disappeared into a small bedroom. Returned with a woolen blanket that he draped over Hazelwood's lower half. The imprisoned man took another swing at him and this time landed it against Foreman's gut. The old man grunted in pain and dropped to a knee. The CEO had been quick and strong, but bound as he was, there could be no second move.

Foreman took his time rising. After he had collected himself, he motioned to the tin cup. "I assume you ain't drinking this tonight then?"

"Fuck yourself, old man. You come close to me again, I'll kill you."

Foreman removed the tin cup from the table and set it beside the stove. Then he approached Hazelwood again, this time circling behind the secured man. He checked the duct tape that joined Hazelwood to the chair. Then, moving to Hazelwood's indefensible side, he punched his prisoner twice in the face, making the legs of the chair teeter each time. He found the roll of duct tape and went to the man again and bound his free hand so that he was utterly immobilized. Then he stepped away to consider the man's bruised face, his blackened lips, the missing tooth. Foreman tore a length of the tape from the roll and palmed it securely over Hazelwood's mouth.

Then he shut off the lights, blew out the lamps, and fell into his bed in the next room over. He dreamt of his wife, of her hands at their sink, washing orange carrots in the afternoon sunlight. He dreamt of her laughing, of her face shining with happiness and the glow of summertime, but in the dream, he could not hear her laughter or her voice. His dreams were always without soundtracks.

HOUR EIGHTEEN

Foreman woke to the nearby sound of wood scraping against wood. Four pegs walking. He sat up in bed to find Hazelwood suddenly beside him, still bound, eyes wide, the tape gone from over his mouth and now replaced with a steak knife clenched between his jaws. Foreman jerked his feet loose of the bedsheets and scissored a kick to the CEO's face, sending the knife clattering to the floor. Another series of blows tipped Hazelwood wobbling slowly over.

"Let me go, you old fuck! Let me the hell go! Let me go!"

Foreman was out of breath, his nerves well rattled, his old heart beating uncontrollably. He grabbed his chest.

The businessman laughed. "You dumb old bird. This how you want to go out? Over this? A little oil spilt? Some fucking birds, some whales, a couple of dolphins? Some shrimp some fat fuck can't eat at Red Lobster for a few months? You going to kill me, old man? Over oil? Over some fucking oil." Hazelwood was overturned, his face on the floor, his feet blue, the toenails ravaged with his effort.

Foreman sat on the bed and breathed deeply, his hand on his chest. He looked down at the man bound to the chair.

Behind the overturned chair, four erratic grooves in the floors marked the crippled progress of the CEO into his bed-chamber.

"My die has been cast," Foreman said at last. "This planet. It's worth a hell of a lot more than any of us. Oil ain't worth dying for. But this planet sure as hell is. And I want it known that I tried my best, that I didn't give up or shrug my shoulders. I believe that."

"You've been reading too much poetry. You sound like an old faggot."

They stayed that way for some time, looking at each other, their hearts racing, sunlight careening through the windows and outside the birds singing and deer moving in the shad-ows. The old man began coughing, tasted his own blood and bile, last night's meal not sitting well in his fragile gut.

"You're safe enough here, anyway," Foreman said. He pulled a duvet over the fallen man until it covered him like a tarpaulin. "I better head into town. Make things look normal."

He moved unsteadily into the kitchen, made coffee, drank water. His hands shaking apart.

HOUR TWENTY

The little town teemed with police, unmarked cars, tele-vision crews. The main street packed with automobiles, vans, strange pedestrians in suits and ties and skirts and high heels. Foreman drove slowly, hands loose on the wheel of the old truck as he gaped at the ruckus. His legs trembled in his trousers. If they were not already looking, they would be looking soon. He pulled into a parking space and sat a moment collecting himself. He would spend the day in town being seen.

He left the truck and pulled his barn jacket tight. He had lost so much weight that it felt more like a robe of tattered canvas. The wind seemed to pass through his body as if his flesh were gauze. He knew he would not make it to see the end of winter, and maybe not even the beginning. He shuffled down the sidewalk.

In the post office, to one side of the counter, a television woman was interviewing Father Malloy. The priest was praying for the CEO, calling for forgiveness. A light was attached to the camera aimed at the priest and the light shone so brightly as to make Malloy's skin translucent as milk. Foreman knew Malloy and had never trusted him. The priest's hands too soft for Foreman's liking. The priest that had shepherded the town prior had been a miner in his youth, who split five cords of wood every autumn before the snow began flying. That priest had hands covered in sandpaper and leather. Hands like paws. Rumors abounded that in his mining days, he could beat all comers at arm wrestling. He'd had a beard that seemed full of the magic of God. Black eyes. You did not want to sin because something in his countenance made you believe that he knew your sins and would wrestle them out and away from you. Beat them out of you, if necessary. Absolve and redeem and make you repent, weeping like a scared child. This new priest looked like a spy. Foreman gathered his mail and left. There wasn't much—a few sweepstakes circulars and some catalogues addressed to his wife. Sad little reminders of her.

He walked across the street to the town's only café. It was crowded. Unable to sit beside the bay windows, he took a seat at the counter, where the loggers, farmers, and old men sat. He ordered toast and coffee. His stomach was upset. He drank slowly, the hot coffee in his belly warming him.

A logger he knew leaned in, said, "Truth is, I don't give two shits if some rich bastard gets lost in the woods, wanders off. Fuck him. Should've packed some expensive Gore-Tex. Some fancy wool. Shit. Could've thrown some locals some money. Hired a guide."

"Amen," said Foreman. "Well, they think they're indestructible, bulletproof. They think they know everything."

"I heard a report on the news," said the logger, "that there was enough oil down there to fill Yankee Stadium. Maybe more. Who'll ever know? Goddamn travesty. Fucker should've been hung, is what should have happened. But it don't work like that, do it? You know the drill. You got money . . . Shit. They set you up at the Club Fed. Probably get shrimp cocktail for dinner, only it don't come out of Galveston, that's for sure."

Foreman nodded. "So he just wandered off then?"

The logger blew his nose in a handkerchief, not managing to remove all the particulate from his mustache. "It don't really make sense to me. The maid showed up at his place and all his shit was still there. Posh car. Luggage. Like he just disappeared. I think he just got himself lost. Fucker left his wallet on the counter next to his keys. They ain't got any idea of anything."

"How long's he been out there?" Foreman asked.

The logger shoveled catsupped eggs into his mouth, shrugged. "Less than a day, they figure. No idea."

They watched the television suspended in a corner of the café. It was surreal, the way the world was seeing their town live. They watched time unspooling before them, turned occasionally to peer at the main street, where the faces broadcast on the TV talked into cameras and microphones. It was dizzying, as if two worlds nearly identical existed just ten seconds or so apart, their actions and drama otherwise almost indistinguishable.

Foreman and the logger sat at the counter a good hour or more. There was nothing else to do. They traded sections of the battered newspaper out of Minneapolis/St. Paul. Played several games of cribbage. *Fifteen two, fifteen four, fifteen six, and pair of sevens for two equals eight.* In the sky, gray clouds scudding quickly and the fallen autumnal leaves tumbling faster than passing cars.

"Snow coming."

"I feel it too. Thought it was the cancer this morning, but maybe it's just the weather."

"Christ, Foreman, I am sorry about that."

Foreman blew on his coffee. "That's kind of you. But it's all right. I'm going to be with my wife."

"She and my mom used to play bridge together. I never heard an unkind word."

Foreman's eyes had suddenly become misty and he looked away from the logger. He said very quietly, "I miss her."

The logger left some money on the Formica counter and touched Foreman's back. "You need anything, don't be afraid to holler."

Foreman nodded and stared into the diner's kitchen. He would wait until dusk before leaving.

HOUR THIRTY

Foreman found Hazelwood where he'd left him, in a pool of his own bright urine, the seat of his pants filled with shame. The man was broken and weeping, shivering. Foreman dragged him toward the fieldstone hearth, then began working quickly, balling up a few sheets of newspaper, building a structure of wood and paper intermingled with twigs and kindling and pinecones. He struck a match and touched the paper with fire. He blew on the little flames tenderly, coaxing them to climb the ladders of wood. He tore curls of birch bark from the woodbin and added them to the fire.

"I'm so cold," Hazelwood complained. "I shat myself."

"You know the deal," Foreman said. "Drink up and we're

done. I told you, I'd even cut it. How do you guys say it? I'd blend it."

"I'm so goddamn thirsty."

Foreman warmed his palms and felt the fire through his garments.

"What if I change?" Hazelwood asked. "What if I make a public apology?" He snuffled. "There has to be another way! I've got a wife. Three kids! I've got pictures—take a look—on my phone. Please! Please!"

"About your telephone," said Foreman. He went outside briefly, came back in. In the palm of his old hand, the destroyed components of the telephone. "You never know," said Foreman. "I thought maybe they could track you or something. Technology such as it is these days." He tossed the wrecked cellular into the fire, then stood from the hearth and went to the kitchen. He poured himself a glass of water and watched Hazelwood. Against the windowpanes, stars of snow sizzling briefly and then expiring.

HOUR THIRTY-FOUR

Both of them at the table, their eyes locked. Between them the tin cup, and outside a November blizzard come down out of Alberta and through Saskatchewan and the Dakotas. The winds shook the cabin and the fire in its place wheezed and snapped.

"This ain't going to help your cause," said Foreman.

The other man was now dying too, if only a little. He continuously licked his blackened lips, but there was no moisture left inside the hole of his mouth to lubricate anything. His lips had grown chapped too. "I'm so thirsty," he said in what was now a tragic loop.

"These early storms are sometimes the worst. Heavy snow full of moisture. The plows not yet ready. The salt trucks not loaded. People not used to driving through such conditions. No chains on their tires. They ain't gonna find you in time now. It's all up to you. You got to drink up. Pay the piper. You drink from that tin cup and I'll give you all the water you can drink. Wine even. Feed you. Take you straight away to the hospital in Duluth. I give you my word on that. But I ain't budging on this thing, either. We're here together now, you and me. And if we both die, we both die, and I am at peace with that."

Foreman stood from the table and went to the refrigerator. Came back with a glass of water and an apple. He ate the apple slowly, chewing its skin, his old teeth biting into the white meat of the fruit. He looked out into the storm and watched the swirling of billions of flakes, watched drifts gathering at the bases of young balsams. He would have to go out at least once during the evening to start the truck and charge the battery. He would take every precaution. There were two pairs of snowshoes in the bed of the vehicle and chocolate and brandy in the glove box. Candles and matches and extra clothing and an ancient blanket.

"Honeycrisp is my favorite apple. The best acidity. Cleans your mouth right out."

The cabin was quiet then. Foreman's chewing and the fire's spare music.

Hazelwood said, "My wife drank oil one time." The bound man seemed to hang from his perch, his body leaning forward, head bowed.

Foreman stopped chewing a moment and then continued, watching Hazelwood.

"Our first child was overdue. Just didn't want to come out. And my wife, she wanted to do things the old-fashioned way. No drugs during the birth. She's crazy. I mean, I love her, but she's crazy. You two might get along." He shook his head, worked his captive hands in their knots. "The midwife gave her castor oil. I remember that now. Mixed it with a little orange juice. She drank it all down. I remember that. Never complained. Meredith was born about an hour later. In the bathtub. You know what that stuff does? It irritates the bowels, I guess. And that in turn stimulates the uterus. I took a sip. It was awful. I'll never forget.

"You never had children, did you?" asked Hazelwood, looking up now at his captor.

Foreman gnawed at the apple and glowered at his prisoner.

"I bet it makes it a helluva lot easier for you to kill me, doesn't it? Without having kids of your own? Without knowing what it means to be a father? Without anyone to embarrass or to take the shame of what you've done. You fucking environmentalists. Living in the abstract. Your goddamn hearts are two sizes bigger than your heads."

Foreman threw the core of his apple square at Hazelwood's face. "Eat that."

Hazelwood stayed cool. "You think I'd do something to leave this planet worse for my kids? You think I'd do that? Knowingly? How could I face them? It wasn't my fault. I'm just a man. One goddamn man."

"Why ain't I surprised that a CEO is sitting before me shirking the responsibility, rather than standing up and trying to change things, to make things better. You fuckwads get paid big money to sit before Congress without a recollection of a thing, to smile into the camera and lie, to find new ways to bilk people. Push comes to shove, you're salesmen. Plain and simple."

And then they glared at each other for hours, the tin cup between them still full of its patient blackness. Foreman glanced at his old nicked wristwatch. Midnight; a new day. He stood from the table, bent down for the thrown apple core and went out into the blizzard to run the truck, charge the battery. Two feet of snow on the ground heavy and wet as new cement not yet hardened. He sat in the truck with his eyes on the cabin. He could see the top of a leg of Hazelwood's chair and he could see that the chair wasn't moving. He turned the heater up and sat in the flowing warmth until the heat of the engine had melted the carpeting of snow that had obscured the truck in whiteness. Then he cut the engine and went back inside.

"No blanket tonight," Foreman told Hazelwood. Then he dragged the man's chair into the bathroom and kicked him over. "I'm locking this bathroom. Wake me up when you're ready to drink. I'll hear you."

HOUR FORTY-TWO

Foreman woke up, his bladder full and burning. Outside: the world seemingly erased and made anew. Everywhere: whiteness and snow yet falling from the well-obscured sky. A strange sound coming from the bathroom. The old man shuffled quickly to the locked door. His key in the knob, he tried to press into the room but he could feel the CEO resisting. The door slightly ajar, Foreman could see that Hazelwood had somehow forced himself up at one point and drank from the porcelain toilet bowl. The front of his cashmere sweater, already ruined by oil, now also a V of dampness. His back was against a low cabinet and his feet pressed against the door, still taped up to his chair.

Foreman said, "You quit this shit or I'll break your motherfuckin' legs!"

Hazelwood relaxed his legs after a moment and the door caromed open. The oil magnate was laughing through his missing front tooth, his gums and teeth slightly less black. "I pissed all over your floor," he said. "I drank for hours. Best water I ever had."

Foreman jerked the man and chair out of the room and

across the house, their path delineated by marks across the wooden floorboards. Foreman dragged him outside, kicked him down a small set of stairs, and let the man come to rest in a dune of snow. The old man went back inside. He had been beaten again. Tore at his scalp, the flyaway hair.

"Dumb," he said to himself. "Dumb, dumb, dumb."

HOUR FORTY-THREE

Near hypothermic, Hazelwood was incoherent. Foreman pulled him back inside and set him beside the fire. The captive man smelled awful. Foreman had been unprepared for any of his own failings, and unprepared as well for the fortitude of this captain of industry, the man's resolve. He smacked the back of the man's cold head and the contact felt good, so he hit him again. Then Foreman slunk into a chair and stared at his willful hostage.

HOUR FORTY-FIVE

"The idea come to me one day, not long after the spill," Foreman said. "I was thinking about my childhood and this memory come to me unbidden. It popped right into my head, like a bubble. And I remembered how when I was a little boy, maybe four or five, my daddy was furious with me. It was because I kept shitting my pants. And I guess he thought I was too old for that. It embarrassed him or something."

Hazelwood looked up at his keeper, his face dull, smudged.

"And what I remembered was this time in the kitchen, in the kitchen of the home where I grew up. And I'm sitting at this table. This table right here. Only I'm a little boy. And my grandpa is there too because he's telling my daddy what to do. He's saying, *Make him eat that shit. That'll stop it. Make him eat it.*

"And then I remember that they put my diaper in front of me. Me sitting in a chair, but I was small, so my eyes were about level with the table, with the diaper, and it was a terrible one, overflowing, and it smelled something awful and then my grandpa dropping a spoon into it and saying, *Do it. He ain't no baby anymore, it's his own goddamned mess.* And my daddy holding my face and that spoon and me thinking, Please don't make me. Please don't make me eat my own mess. Please, Daddy. I remember them pushing my face toward it. My own diaper. And I remember that my mom was in the kitchen and I couldn't understand why she didn't stop them. Why didn't she stop them?"

He gazed out the window, drumming this thumbs against the table, Hazelwood watching him.

"So that's what this is about," Hazelwood finally said. "You want me to eat my own shit? Some sick revenge fantasy. Some twisted revenge against your father, maybe authority figures in general?"

Foreman said, "Maybe."

HOUR FORTY-SEVEN

Hazelwood had been smiling at Foreman for an hour, his face and spirits oddly revived.

"You ready?" Foreman asked.

"Bring me over there," Hazelwood said. "I'm going to beat you at your own game. And then I'm sending you to prison. I've decided not to kill you. Nope. I'm going to send you to prison and keep you alive and in pain for a long time. By the end, if your wife is watching from heaven, she won't even want you." He spat on the floor and began hopping the chair on his own toward the table. "Free my fucking hand," he ordered.

Foreman obliged and set the tin cup in front of Hazelwood, then sat down and watched, eyes wide.

Hazelwood raised the cup to his lips now and drank two big gulps. He gagged and held his free hand over his mouth, but spit most of the oil right back out, much of it running down his chin and neck. Some of it sprayed onto Foreman's face and clothing.

"I can't!" gasped Hazelwood. "Christ, it's down my throat. I need water!"

Foreman's chair clattered over as he stood up abruptly. He seized the tin cup and held it to Hazelwood's lips. "Drink! Drink, goddamn it!" Hazelwood choked and Foreman held his nose. The man's throat pumped and then he gagged again and vomited a terrible black mess. Both their faces: masks of black oil and terror. Hazelwood gagging and

143

coughing. Foreman standing over his prisoner, Hazel-wood's free hand now on Foreman's thigh in protest and agony.

"Goddamn it!" Hazelwood roared. "Get that shit out of my mouth! I can't do it! I can't!" He spat and spat, looking terrified now, all slick and black, so different than when Fore-man had first seen his face on television, sea spray threat-ening to dampen his yachting clothes, a martini glass held jauntily above and against the legions of Atlantic waves while he laughed like a man who owned the world. And then Fore-man thought of the images he had seen of the Gulf. The oil-slicked birds. The pods of dolphins. Turtles dead in their shells. Millions of dead fish afloat. He settled into his chair. Studied the oil left in the tin cup. Remembered a vacation with his wife, dolphins racing the bow of the little charter boat that skipped them over the Caribbean. How he'd never seen a dolphin before.

"No deal," said Foreman. "But I'll get you some water. You earned it." He set a glass of artesian water before Ha-zelwood, who drank lustily.

"Get me a goddamn rag! Something to wipe out my mouth," raged Hazelwood. "For chrissakes!"

Foreman retrieved a rag for the man and watched as Ha-zelwood worked the cloth inside his mouth, over his teeth and gums and cheeks. Foreman set three slices of buttered bread before Hazelwood. The man ate ravenously, glaring at Foreman.

"There's still oil in that cup," said Foreman.

"Fuck you. I drank what I could. I can't do any more."

"Well. Here we are."

But the old man was tired and did not know if he could carry out the one thing he had thought himself capable of finishing. There was a tinge of something inside him that questioned what he had begun in the first place. He knew that if the man finished the oil he would have to take him to the hospital and feared that the man might receive more sympathy than punishment from the outside. He could imagine all of those cameras from downtown following Hazelwood, zeroing in on the concerned faces of his wife and children. Foreman stared at Hazelwood. The man covered in oil, only the whites of his eyes bright. Foreman looked at his own clothing, also ruined. They sat looking at each other again, panting. But there was no other course for Foreman, either, and he knew it.

"You know what bothered me most about that spill?" Foreman said.

"I don't give a shit, you sick old fuck. I really don't."

"Loons. They're my favorite birds. Prehistoric things. You know their bones are solid, not hollow, like other birds. Makes them less buoyant so they can swim underwater. Disappear for minutes sometimes. We had a game, my wife and I. A loon would go underwater and we'd try to predict where it would surface. We used to sit out on that porch and listen to the loons sing. It's an eerie sound, and beautiful. It don't sound like anything else. Well, I ain't a birder or nothing, but I'll tell you something. Loons don't winter here. They migrate. Down to the Gulf. They're soon to head down there. And I can't imagine what they'll see or think. I hope they come back up here, but the truth is, I'll be gone anyway, I suppose.

"I don't have much to live for anymore. The planet gets worse and worse, if you ask me, and nobody does anything about it. So I don't know. Maybe it is worth it. To kill you. To put you down. To be the one who sends you away for all times. Because I don't believe that you do care. I don't think you'd know a loon from a flamingo. I don't think you care about them whales or dolphins, and I suspect you could give two shits for those shrimpers and fishermen down there. But they're people too. With kids and wives. What are they going to do? Take your dirty blood money? Take your money and shut up? Go work at a Walmart. Greeting shoppers, maybe. *Hullo, my name is Dan, and I used to be a captain of a boat. Employed four guys. Brought dinner home every night fresh out of the ocean. Calluses on my hands. I used to smell like the sea. You have a nice fucking time shopping today. Buy a new TV. Buy some ice cream for those kids. Some toilet paper.*"

Hazelwood spat black.

"I don't know anymore about anything," said Foreman. "Like I said, I used to be a monkey wrencher. A goddamned sabot. I blew up a dam one time. It was beautiful. All that water gone out in one big rush. The river free and unbound.

I'll never forget that. Other than marrying my wife, it was probably the best thing I ever did. Sitting on the riverbank, watching that water go where it wanted to go."

He lowered his head, scratched the remaining fibers that clung to his scalp. He glanced outside and the snow was still falling, though more slowly now—the snow of the cinema. Foreman opposite him at the table, spitting oil onto the floor. The fire had died out and their breaths were visible inside the cabin.

"I'm cold," said Hazelwood. "I can't feel my feet. I can't feel my fucking feet."

HOUR FIFTY-FIVE

Foreman and Hazelwood beside the revived fire, the prisoner wiggling his feet close to the flames, a puzzled look on his face.

"I'm moving them, but I can't feel anything."

Foreman was reading a slim volume of haiku, his thick reading glasses balanced on his nose. He did not look away from his book.

"I think this tape is too tight," Hazelwood said. "I can't feel my toes."

Foreman licked his fingers as he turned the brittle pages. The fire crackled on.

"Back in college, I studied archaeology," said Hazelwood.

"But there weren't any jobs in that field, so I began getting frustrated just before I graduated. I wasn't always rich. But then, the spring break before I graduated, a big oil company sponsored a trip for us. We visited four digs out west. Utah, Montana, New Mexico, and Arizona. The oil company covered everything. Our bus, our food, our lodgings. We stayed in cheap motels, but it was great, we didn't know any better. I couldn't've been more than twenty-one, twenty-two. Watching TV in some motel room and drinking warm beer and smoking cigarettes. One of the best times in my life."

Foreman had turned from his book.

"Well, at the end of the trip, this executive gets onto our bus and we gave him a round of applause. He was an alum of our college, so we immediately liked him even though he was this rich old fucker. But he encouraged us to all apply for jobs at his company. Said that we had similar skills to the geologists they hired. That he liked hiring archaeologists because that was what he had studied. So that's what I did. That fall I was in Houston for my training. Then they shipped me off to Saudi Arabia. To the North Sea. It was great. It was how I saw the world. They took good care of me. They really did."

He spat into the fire and the fire jumped. He smiled darkly.

Hazelwood looked right at Foreman now. "I swear to you, I am not a bad person," he said. "I am *not* a bad person." And then: "My stomach is burning. I can feel that."

He looked back into the fire and Foreman returned to his poems.

HOUR FIFTY-SIX

Hazelwood hopped his chair away from the fire and began shuffling it toward the old, stained immigrant table. Foreman regarded him from beside the hearth. It took the CEO a good two minutes to cross the small room. When he was finally beside the table he snatched the tin cup and drank the remaining oil down in one quick gulp. Then he clutched his own throat and began gagging again, only this time there was no vomit. He could not even make a scream of protestation. Foreman moved from his chair into the kitchen and poured a tall glass of water, held it to the man's blackened lips. Hazelwood drank quickly and then spit the water out and oil came too, though only a little.

"A rag," he said hoarsely.

Foreman found a fresh handkerchief and held Hazelwood's head, swabbed out his mouth for him. The man had gone very pale and his body was convulsing.

"Son of a bitch," said Foreman, and he went out into the falling snow and turned the truck over, its engine revving, black smoke coughing out the tailpipe. He turned the heat on high. "Son of a bitch did it."

He went back into the cabin and wrapped the man in

blankets and carried him to the truck, laying him across the bench seat. "I'll get you there," Foreman said. "I promised I would." Though now he was afraid. The gravel drive to the cabin was buried under three feet of snow and there were no chains on the truck's tires. He wondered if there was enough weight in the bed of the truck. He'd thought that he had taken every precaution. He felt, in that moment, a murderer.

He pressed the gas pedal lightly and the truck lurched into the confusion of snow, pressing its front bumper into the wilderness of white, only to refuse further progress. He slid the truck into reverse and went back over their tracks. This time he pressed the gas pedal down a little farther. They went up and over a drift, the truck settling onto a plain of snow like a misbegotten raft, the tires resting on nothing but a drift of snow that offered no purchase.

"Oh, Jesus," Foreman said. "Oh, I am sorry, brother. Sorry, sorry, sorry." He slammed the gas pedal, but there was no traction now, just the melt and slide of snow beneath hot rubber. "Oh, goddamn, Hazel, I'll get it. I'll get us out. I'll get you there. I promised you, you son of a bitch."

Foreman slung out of the truck and into the snow, already crotch-deep, but saw that it was fruitless. He reached into the bed of the truck for the snowshoes and then realized he would need only one pair. Hazelwood was passed out, a rivulet of sweet light crude issuing from his mouth onto the fabric of the seat. Foreman quickly strapped on the shoes and pulled the dying man from the truck. Then he stopped, afraid he would not be able to reload him back in. He pushed Hazelwood back into the warmth of the truck. Foreman slapped at the man's face until his eyelids fluttered open, took a handful of snow and held it to Hazelwood's face and neck, let the snow melt on the man. "Wake up!" he said. "Wake up!"

Hazelwood looked at him dimly.

"That oil could kill you, but I think it's too early. You got time. We can *make* it, goddamn it. Stick with me. Wake the fuck up. You got to get back to your family! Your goddamn family! Wake up, Hazel!"

The CEO pulled himself up on the bench seat, still woozy.

"You're going to drive out of here," said Foreman. "I'm going to make you a path."

He shut the door to the truck and moved back to the cabin for a shovel. He came back to the truck with tire chains and a large scoop-bladed shovel. He began digging beneath the tires, sweat pouring off his face. Steadily the truck lowered itself to the earth as Foreman shoveled and the truck's own heat evaporated snow beneath it. Worked the chains on the tires and then Foreman got in front of the truck and began shoveling out two paths, two grooves in the deep white snow. Their spot on earth still many miles from town. The night an impenetrable wasteland. Their going, futile.

Foreman leaned against his shovel, dripping.

Hazelwood at the wheel, whispering *Every precaution, every precaution, every precaution.*

HOUR SIXTY-SIX

Morning, the world absolved, bathed in white. Little birds in the boughs of the pine trees. The sky so blue, the sun still hidden behind the forest, white and yellow. The two men at the table, asleep in their chairs.

Foreman awoke first, so sore from the frantic shoveling he was almost unable to rise. He went to the hearth, began to build a new fire, perhaps his last. He let the heat unwind the pain in his hands. Hazelwood snoring, but there at least, hunched over on his chair, asleep beside the hearth, and alive. Foreman shuffling over to the stove, pouring water into a kettle for coffee, measuring grounds, lighting the burner. He watched Hazelwood sleep. He would put the man back together, see him to the hospital and away.

Foreman cracked eggs into a cast-iron frying pan, breaking the shells against the lip of the pan. In another pan, bacon popping and the smell of its grease in the air. Hazelwood lifted his head. The CEO looked like hell.

"I have to shit," he said. "That oil. It's like my wife." He ran into the bathroom.

They ate together at the old table, newly stained black with Gulf oil.

"I'm going to get you fed," Foreman said. "We're going to drink some coffee, get your strength back in you, and then we're going to hope like hell a plow has come for that outer road. The driveway, I think, might be impassable. But at least we can get you to the road."

Hazelwood nodded, ate ravenously. He was gaining color in his face again. He did not look at Foreman.

They watched water drip from the eaves, the day warming, the sun climbing back to its throne. Two pots of coffee, a pound of bacon, a brick of cheese, a half-dozen eggs. Hazelwood scurrying into the bathroom every hour, returning, eating more. At noon he looked at Foreman, as if sizing the old man up. "I'd like to borrow some clothes. I don't want my kids seeing me like this. The way I smell."

Foreman nodded. They moved around each other warily.

They tried the old truck, but the going was impossible. At last Foreman took a map from the glove compartment and spread it across the old rusty hood. He pointed to a small blue speck and a broken brown line on the map and said, "You're here, all right? You see this. It's an old logging road. That's at the end of the driveway. Get on that road and it'll take you just outside of town. Take this," he said, pushing the map into Hazelwood's chest. "Point out where you come from to the cops. They'll know where to come."

Foreman gave Hazelwood a pair of snowshoes, his parka, mittens, and a wool hat. A thermos of coffee and a backpack of food and supplies. "Go on," he said, "you outlasted me. Get the fuck out of here before I change my mind. Go. Or I'll just shoot you."

Hazelwood eyed him, moving backward awkwardly in the shoes, the snow sticky and heavy. Foreman turned his back to the man and went back inside the cabin, sat at the table and looked outside. Then he stood, took a bottle of wine, uncorked it, and drank without a cup until his teeth were a dark purple.

HOUR SEVENTY

Evening clouds drooping down close to the snow-burdened balsams and the spreading crowns of the white pines. The old floorboards slick with gasoline and oil, kerosene from the lamps and lanterns. The dying widower hunched over at the table with a box of matches, the main room of the cabin pungent with fumes, though dark. No lights. The white of the earthbound snow enough light for the old man's failing eyes to see that there was nothing left to do but what he had all along intended and thought to be right.

He struck the sulfur of the match tip and held the little flame in his hand for a moment before flinging it into the darkness. And then he waited at the table, drinking water from his favorite glass, the tin cup now empty except for its own little lake of fire. His body growing hot, little flames dancing near his shoes, his trouser legs.

CODA

Sirens and the strobe of blue, red, and white lights through a winter forest, plows leading the parade, pushing the snow to the sides of the backcountry roads. The missing person, the CEO, in the town's only motel, guarded by two state troopers, his wife en route from Duluth.

Ahead of the police cruisers, the forest begins to glow yellow and red, and then they smell smoke. The driveway is too narrow for the state plows, so the police and SWAT leave their vehicles and come high-stepping through the snow, their assault rifles held high, a few dogs pulling at their leashes, fangs bared, slobbering white bubbles. The driveway is a long corridor of white, overhung by snow-burdened tree branches. They move through the tunnel of boughs toward the fire, which is loud and huge. Already the cabin is falling in upon itself.

They find the truck, chains on the tires, the shovel abandoned. They watch the flames jump up to threaten the boughs of a huge white pine. They listen as windows and glasses and china explode. They stand back farther. They begin looking for prints, tracks in the snow. Some sign of escape. But there are no tracks to be found.

And in the night their sirens, and far off, a pack of wolves. The ice of the little pond creaking in the cold and a house on fire.

IN WESTERN COUNTIES

HER FACE HAD BEEN MADE into a jigsaw puzzle. Aida saw how the poor girl tried to hide the scars: the cake makeup, the masking hands, the long hair and baseball cap. The edges of the puzzle pieces purple and crudely lined. Her mouth crooked, but somehow sweet. She smiled painfully at Aida. Pushed an envelope of money across the sticky surface of the café table. The envelope was not thick; it was all that the scarred woman had left.

The restaurant was abandoned. The waitress hovered around them, refilled their mugs, nodded gamely at Bethany. Said to her, "These are on me." Then leaned into the table, wiped the surface with her bleachy rag and said, "There's a way out. Always is. I been there too. Don't let him beat you like that. You'll be dead inside a year by the look of it."

Some of the fortitude seemed to leak out of Bethany and

she deflated slightly, set her mug down, and readjusted the bill of her cap. She looked up at the waitress and said, "God bless you." But Aida could see that she didn't believe in God at all, that her eyes contained only anger and fear.

The waitress nodded and then went away, near the coffee urn, where she watched them, sometimes kibitzing with the cook, a pock-faced man with a long ponytail who peered out at the two women from behind the heating elements glowing red and orange.

They sat for a while, saying nothing, glancing all around the café, and then Aida said, "Let's go outside, then," taking Bethany by the elbow and gently lifting her up. She took the money and stuffed it into her jacket. Hoped she would remember it was there. She was always losing things, so many things.

They went to Aida's truck, an old F-150. Aida opened the door and guided Bethany onto the bench seat. She went around behind the truck and looked at the woman's slumped shoulders framed in the rear window. *Bethany,* she reminded herself. With her long finger, she wrote the name in the palm of her hand, making the calloused skin go white where the letters were: BETHANY. She wrote the name again in the dirt and dust that clung to the metal of her truck: BETHANY. There were chains in the bed of the truck and a tire iron. A spare tire, a bag of last year's autumn leaves, and two cement blocks.

Aida was not in the habit of driving the truck. That morning, en route to Red Wing, she forgot where the knob for the headlights was. She'd just retired from the state highway patrol after twenty-five years and was accustomed to driving a police cruiser. She kicked the gravel. Hail was in the forecast and she waited for it to hit, the violence of the blue-white pellets. She got inside the truck, slamming the door. Bethany shuddered.

"I'm tired of it," Bethany said. "Tired! He does this to me, but there ain't anything for me to do. Nothing to do to make him stop! Goddamn it!" She beat her fist into the dashboard.

Aida rolled down her window and withdrew a package of cigarettes from her jean jacket. Offered the package over to Bethany, who shook her head. Aida rarely smoked, but just now needed the fire and smoke to fill the silence she was incapable of filling herself. She took a Zippo lighter from the glove box and lit the cigarette, inhaled deeply. Still no hail, but the sky was yellowing, the clouds scudding quickly, oddly no wind to rile the ditch grass. It was late in the year for hail. Bethany's outburst apparently over, they sat again in silence. Beyond the café and the highway running past it: a barbed wire fence, the concrete skeleton of an abandoned silo, the stone footings of a bygone barn. Then just blue and yellow sky and rapidly circulating clouds. Aida's ears popped, the pressure changing.

"All right," Aida said, her voice husky and sandpapery, "what do you want me to do?"

Bethany stared back at her pitifully. She had once been attractive. The huge blue eyes, a thick rope of brown hair.

Her skin otherwise alabaster, perfect. Aida could see how quickly the bravery came and went in her face, how the strength was braided together with rage, and how Bethany was most cogent when the memory of her attack resurfaced and she needed to strike out and *be* her anger. All the violence that had preceded her mauling.

"You know what I want you to do?" Bethany said. "I want you to get him. And I don't care what you do as long as you understand that I want my revenge. You look at my face if you need a reminder of what I want you to do. And don't take him to your friends in the police, either. 'Cause we already know that ain't going to help." Her voice quaked. Aida squinted behind the smoke and dimly remembered that her old colleagues would not be of any assistance. She felt something in her chest like remorse, the knowledge that she had failed this woman, Bethany, before. *Bethany, Bethany, Bethany.*

"Is he out there?" Aida asked. "On that farm?"

Bethany seemed to shake her head just slightly, as if she could not understand how Aida had forgotten some crucial detail. It was a politely confounded expression she had seen on more and more faces of late, and it frustrated her. It had been her job to look strong, to appear inscrutable.

"Do you need to write this stuff down?" Bethany asked.

"I'll take care of it," Aida said, breathing out smoke. "No, I'll take care of it. But you need to leave town for a while. I'll take you to the Greyhound station and then you have to go away. I don't care where."

The hail hit miles away from the bus station, and they

pulled over under a bridge crumbling and rusted. Swallows swooping in and out of their nests. They watched the hail bounce off the asphalt. Ping-Pong balls of ice out on the road. They rolled down the windows and felt the cold in the air. Aida opened up her door and slid out, stood underneath the last vestige of protection that the bridge provided. She collected a stone of hail from the ground and held it in her palm, then watched as it melted away. She drank the remaining water. Far away she saw a conical cloud lower toward the ground, but it never did touch and after a while it seemed to lose steam, retreating back up into the heavens. Then the sun reappeared, and a rainbow broke extravagantly across the sky, deep-toned and immense.

They drove over the hail-strewn road toward the city of Albert Lea and the Greyhound depot, nothing more than a glass room attached to a Shell gas station. There were old magazines on tables near the big windows and a view of the prairie and passing eighteen-wheelers. Two children were pounding the Plexiglas of a vending machine where a candy bar hung on a thin spiral of aluminum. Their little fists and bodies unable to shake the machine adequately. Bethany punched the squat rectangle once and the chocolate bar fell into an awaiting trough. The children snatched the bar and then looked up into her face, as if to thank her, but their own diminutive faces fell apart and they ran away, outside the waiting room. Aida watched as they ran across the parking lot to a woman—their mother, she guessed—and pointed back at the stranger with the hideous face.

In front of the idling bus Aida handed Bethany the envelope of money. "You hold on to this until I'm done," she said. "Better you pay me when I finish things up." *I've been losing so many things.*

Bethany nodded, clutched the money, shoved it back into her purse, and boarded the bus. A few minutes later, the bus driver rolled a placard in the window to DULUTH and drove off. Bethany's mutilated face in the window, looking out, her hand pressed to the glass.

He fought dogs in an old barn out on the prairie. Had stolen the land from a widow. He came to her house before dusk, smiling in the glow of the porch light, ignoring the moths powdering his face. She answered the door with a shotgun. He told her that he was her nephew, from Butte, Montana, come with money to buy the family farm. He waved a wad of paper in the air, two fifties on the outsides and nothing in between but thin cardboard coupons for car washes. She looked at him warily, rubbed her forehead as if to loosen out a memory. She undid the lock, lowered the weapon, let him in.

He had watched her for a few weeks from the road with a pair of binoculars. Knew that she rarely left the house and that she lived alone. Knew she was frail. He'd gleaned too that she was senile: she talked to herself incessantly and he had seen her feeding invisible chickens, broadcasting seeds from her hands to nothing but the sparse grass and gravel of her yard. In other cities he had lived in trailer courts or apartment buildings, but inevitably his neighbors complained about the dogs. Their barking, their waste, their potential for violence. He knew he needed privacy and space. The widow's name was Ione Miller. He knew this from stealing her mail.

She served him stale cookies and reheated coffee. He pretended to eat, spit the cookies into a napkin, wiped off his tongue. At the kitchen table he let her talk for two hours, the darkness of the house closing in around them. Then he produced a document that he had her sign, his hand on her frail wrist. She fell asleep in the chair later and he carried her up a flight of stairs to her bed. She weighed next to nothing. When he held a pillow over her face, she did not struggle, her hands swatting weakly at his wrists, as if shooing flies. He pressed his ear to her chest and held a mirror before her thin lips, terrified of her bony fingers reanimating.

And then he went outside to his truck, where he let the three dogs out, kissing at them and clapping his hands. They wagged their tails in the darkness and urinated. He reached into the truck and illuminated the headlights. They shone out onto the prairie, its grasses bending with the evening wind. In the distance, one giant oak. He set off across the field, the dogs at his heels. He collected fallen limbs until dawn, stacking the wood behind the house. In the barn he found kerosene and some rotten lumber, which he also assembled behind the house. Exhausted, he went back inside the house, wrapped the old woman in her bedsheets, carried her out to the barn, and then returned to her bedroom, where he fell into her ancient mattress and went instantly to sleep, boots still on, and the dogs staring at him from the floor, where they curled in on themselves, their eyes soft and wet. In the mattress he felt the depressions of where she had slept for so many years, her ghost in bed with him. He considered burning the thing, but did not want to leave behind its ancient metal coils. He would buy a new one. The mattress was loud and lumpy, but he dozed heavily.

The next evening he lighted a huge pyre behind the house on the margins of the prairie. He watched the flames envelop the figure in bedsheets and then returned to the house, where he looked for a television for over an hour before turning on an old record player, the volume of which filled the house and set the dogs to barking. He quickly threw the machine out onto the lawn before retiring to the bedroom, where he pulled the mattress onto the floor. He lay down and the dogs nestled their bodies against his, warming his thighs and belly. Every time he rolled over, the mattress made a sound like dry leaves. He stripped the mattress of its stale sheets, wrapping them around him, and then he fit the mattress into the old woman's closet, shutting the folding doors, the mattress still alive sounding, everywhere the noise of dry papers being rattled. He went back to the dogs on the floor and fell asleep, the flames of the pyre burning wide and high into the night. It would be impossible for anyone to see the black smoke.

In the morning, a pile of hot ash and coals. He kicked the

cinders for bone but saw nothing discernible. The dogs sniffed the air and there was the bouquet of prairie grasses and flowers. Fresh dry summer air being pushed across the flatlands from the Dakotas. He threw a baseball across the fields and the dogs chased it endlessly. The leather of the dirty orb almost torn away, the marks of the dogs' teeth everywhere, dimpling the baseball a thousand times over. He hung the bedsheets out on the line and they whipped in the wind like spinnakers, the dogs nipping at the moving fabric.

Months passed and he collected dogs, training them, hardening them. He rescued them from overburdened kennels and from the houses of parents with small children, the houses of the frail and elderly. He had moved around the country like this, fighting dogs and organizing circuits: Detroit, Cody, Corvallis, Tempe, Tulsa, Des Moines. He had always loved dogs. His parents had let the family Rottweiler sleep in his crib with him.

Bethany first met him at the pet store where she cashiered. She was timid around men, afraid she smelled of dog food and cat litter. She rarely made eye contact with customers, often leaning back against the till to read thick paperback books. Thirty-one years old, and she had made love only once, during the night of her junior prom. And now Bret Kruk was placing his fingers underneath her chin and lifting her startled face to look into his. There was a line behind him, but no one complained or even coughed. He was handsome in a dangerous-looking sort of way, the muscles in him coiled up like a rattlesnake. In bars and restaurants he demanded the best service without so much as raising his voice, just by darkening his face. People seemed to respect him without reason.

"We should go for a walk sometime," he said. "I'm new around here. You could show me around. Meet my dogs. I bet they'd like you." His voice was warm. His fingertips were warm. He smelled of fresh air.

She smiled, wrote down her telephone number for him, her heart bursting with fire, with an inexhaustible supply of love. Hardly remembered to take his money. He pushed an entire cart of dog food into the parking lot, and she watched from inside as he loaded the heavy bags into a red Ram. She was unaccustomed to seeing new vehicles in the parking lot.

Days later they were walking beside Crawfish Creek, not far from his farm. The fields around the great farmhouse lay fallow and there was no manure smell in the air, nor were there any animals in sight—no cows or sheep or even horses—just his dogs. At that time he had three that he favored. They rushed out to greet her car when she pulled beside the farmhouse, teeth bared, tossing creamy slobber over her windows, claws raking the metal of her small Japanese car. She waited for him to come out of the house. He smiled and waved at her. Said something almost inaudibly and the three dogs sat in rapt attention, panting.

"You can get out," he said. "They won't bother you now."

She had brought him a loaf of homemade bread still warm from the oven and steaming its plastic bag like breath. He seemed too tall and skinny, a scarecrow of a man, though well-muscled.

"This is my pack," he said, "or part of it. This is Oso, Point, and Bick."

"Part of it?" she asked, confused.

"I'm a breeder," he said, touching the sinewy muscle of his own biceps where several tattoos had been crudely executed. Cartoon bulldogs.

"Are these pit bulls?" she asked, extending her hand gingerly toward them.

"Don't be afraid," he said forcefully, "it spooks them."

Their long tongues lapped at her fingers. She giggled.

"See?" he said, watching her from the corners of his eyes, "my babies."

"How long have you lived out here?" she asked, rubbing the dogs' ears. There were scars on their heads, some old and some new. She touched the animals lightly, wondering if he had rescued the wounded trio.

"A few months," he said. "My grandmother passed away and left me the land. I never grew up around here, so I'm still learning the roads, where all the stores are at. It's nice enough. Room for the dogs to roam. And I got the barn." He motioned toward the hulking red building, set up off the earth on a foundation of fieldstones. She thought she heard barking in that direction.

"So you have other dogs too?" she asked, frowning.

He shook his head, smiled. "You sure have a lot of questions," he said. "Here. Let's go for a walk." He reached for her hand. His was warm, hers cold and clammy. She was conscious of her own skin on his.

He had packed a picnic basket and they went past the farmhouse and over a field of chopped cornstalks, a year's worth of weeds just beginning to die off. It was October, the air cool and damp. The sky was gray and they marched through the field, his dogs bounding everywhere, happy. Pheasants fluttered loudly into the sky, exploding off the ground, startling her.

"I've been watching you," he said, looking at her face, drawing her eyes up to his. "You're gorgeous. You know that?"

She did not know what to say, so she turned her head away but squeezed his hand with hers. She wanted to believe him but didn't entirely. No one had ever called her gorgeous; no one had ever called her anything. At the top of a ridge the field dropped down below them toward the leaden-colored creek. The leaves on the trees had mostly turned and come down, but some still clung on in russets and gold.

They walked until dusk, returning through the field to the farmhouse. She saw a pile of old ashes behind the house, thought she saw something like a bone. Dismissed it as one of the dog's playthings. Went on. Her feet were tired.

"You could come in," he said. "I'll make you tea."

He held her hands. In the wind, the sound of more barking. She looked toward the barn. She did not want to be alone. "Come on," he said, "I won't bite."

And she followed him inside the farmhouse. Later they made love on an old brass bed. He was gentle at first, then later more rough. Her underwear had remained on one of her legs, like an anklet. Afterward, lying there beside him, she watched as the dogs nosed open the door to the bedroom and stood next to his side of the bed. They looked at him patiently and one of them licked his toes, which were hanging off the bed. She looked across the room at the closet, where a broken mattress stood crookedly, pressing up against the folding doors. Out the window she looked down at the circle of ashes and dead coals. She wondered if someday this might be her own house. She stood up to go to the bathroom and the dogs growled, but she simply shushed them, patted their heads and scratched their bellies. They whined quietly in pleasure.

In the hallway were dozens of black-and-white photographs hanging inside aged wooden frames. Early photographs of farmers, horses, state fairs. Somber faces looking back at a photographer no doubt hidden behind a big box camera, a cape of black wool draped over the man's head and back. *He must feel very connected to this house*, she thought. She touched the glass that protected the photos with her fingers, left her prints on the strangers' faces. She proceeded down the hallway and sat on the toilet. The sound of her own water embarrassed her. The smell of coitus was on her skin, on the smallest of her hairs. She wondered if the dogs understood that fragrance.

Aida had seen Bethany precisely twice before the night she called from the pet store, asking for help. But she remembered only the one occurrence, which even now she could not forget.

Four months shy of her retirement from the highway patrol, the K9 department sent her to the pet store to buy a bag of kibble—a fool's errand, in fact, and she the fool. Her coworkers had simply sent her on a mission to get her away from the station, where they removed her desk from the office, four big officers carrying it into the back recesses of the garage. Following which everyone hurriedly rearranged their own desks to compensate for the empty spot they had left behind. And then they filled her locker with a thousand golf balls, red-faced with laughter and pleasure, while several miles away, she entered the pet store, its smells overwhelming. From the back of the store: the calls and singing of a dozen different exotic birds. She followed the signs, her index finger raised in the air—DOGS—then shouldered the fifty-pound bag and walked back up to the registers. She paused to observe the fish in their aquariums. She had never owned any pets, not even in her childhood.

Kruk was there, had not noticed her, despite her red hair and uniform. His face was buried in the young cashier's hair, near her ear. The cashier was shaking, and then Aida saw that she was weeping, that her face had been mutilated, the wounds still fresh and bleeding. He shook her one final time and then with an open hand smacked her face. Instantly Aida set the bag of kibble down and reached for her service weapon.

"Stop it right there," she said to Kruk's flexed back muscles.

"Mind your fuckin' business," he said to her, hardly even bothering to turn around. "It's all over anyway. Hard to imagine ever wanting to see *this* face again."

Then, taking the older woman in more fully, his eyes flickered in recognition and then he cracked a small smile. *The redhead cop,* he thought. *She doesn't even recognize us. Beth's face.*

"Hands on the back of your head," said Aida.

He complied, folding them slowly over the back of his skull, his close-cropped black hair. There was blood on his fingers.

"On your knees," Aida told him.

The cashier wept loudly, blood dripping down her neck. "Hold on, girl," Aida said. "Call nine-one-one. Call it now."

But the girl did not respond. He was lowering himself onto his knees and Aida went to him, holstering her pistol as she reached for her handcuffs. Only then he rolled slightly forward and to his right, and, grabbing her outstretched hand, threw her over himself, the pistol clattering on the store's shining tiled floor. The store was empty, just the three of them, the manager out delivering the day's bank deposits, with a side trip home to give his diabetic cat a shot of insulin. Kruk seized the weapon and caught Aida in his sights. She raised her hands in the air, her face unmoving. The macaws and parrots shrieked loudly, pantomimed the foul language of teenage customers like a filthy peanut gallery, at once disturbed and delighted by the ruckus.

"Bad idea," she told him, "stupid, stupid idea." She rubbed her head, considered how she had come to lose the pistol. Studied the skinny man in front of her, tattoos on his arms, the aged ink little more than a blur of shapes.

He moved away from the two women, out of the store and into his big shining red truck. Aida was just reaching into her pocket for the keys to her prowler when Bethany caught her arm, the girl's grip surprisingly strong. Her face was bleeding, the scars reopened, and her tears must have burned in those wounds. Aida wanted to shake her off but stopped. Outside, she heard the man's truck burn rubber and disappear.

"Don't," Bethany said. "Just . . . don't."

Aida's mouth opened; she was furious. "He's got my gun!" she shouted. She turned to go, but the bleeding woman held her in place.

"Don't, okay? I don't want to press charges. He didn't steal from the store. All he got was your gun, but I have to tell you something. Please stop. Okay? Just listen to me. All he got was your gun." Then, "You know me. Right? You *know* me. You have to *help* me."

The store was quiet. Even the birds were now mute in their cages.

Aida shook her head and looked harder at the young woman. She seemed familiar. But the wounds, already like scars, the horrible wounds. She would have called for backup but the young woman held her arm so tightly that Aida listened. Twenty years ago she would not have lingered, would have pursued the man all the way to Canada had he run that far north. But now she did stop. She felt so, so weary.

And then Bethany told Aida the story.

She had moved into Bret Kruk's farmhouse. Her meager furniture, her clothing. There was plenty of room for her things among the stale-smelling dressers and cobwebbed closets stinking of mothballs. She cleaned for a week straight. Mopped the sagging old wood floors and washed the drapes and linens. She threw his food away, restocked the monolithic refrigerator with greens, fruits, vegetables. She made bread in the oven. She loved that kitchen, the views of the fields open all around her. She bought a houseplant and named it Ione, the name she had seen written inside one of the dressers and again on one of the photographs in the hallway.

It was a week after she'd moved in that the headlights first came teeming up her driveway, after ten in the evening. At first she thought it was a mob and ran across the farmyard toward the illuminated barn, where a fire was burning outside the structure in a steel drum. He spent a good deal of time out there in the barn with his dogs. She had never been invited inside. Determined to warn him about the impending cars, she pushed the doors open.

He was inside a cage of plywood and barbed wire, screaming at two pit bulls, working them up, their powerful bodies lathered with sweat. He held them apart, his knuckles white on two separate leashes, both of his thin arms cut in sharply defined muscle. All at once he let the leashes go and the dogs leapt at one another. One was dead in moments, the other dog at its throat, blood spraying onto the dirt floor of the barn. She held her hands over her mouth. The loudest sound was Kruk's breathing as he panted over the two dogs, and then restrained the one alive, releasing it. Pulling it away. Whereupon the night erupted in the noise of angry dogs all around them. She saw then that he was not a breeder, and yet even now she could not bring herself to understand what was happening.

"Bret," she said unsteadily, "there are people coming up the driveway."

"Go back inside, baby," he said, his voice too calm for her. "Go back inside, I'm just expecting some visitors."

"They're here," she whispered. Then, "Bret, what is . . . what's *happening*?"

"Go on now," he said. "Go to sleep. Just some bet-making, that's all." He turned his back to her, led the "winning" dog away, toward where she did not know. Help, she hoped. Bandages and medicine, painkillers and water, though all that seemed very unlikely.

The dead dog before him she recognized as Bick. He slept in their bedroom, ran in his dreams. Bret had described his coloring as "red red nosed." Bethany shouldered into the cage, picked up the dog in her arms, its body impossibly hot and heavy, and left the barn, just as a column of men came toward her in the night, their own hands full of leashes, dogs snarling, dogs whimpering, dogs who remained chillingly silent, even happy amidst it all. The night suddenly raw with violence.

She carried the dog into the house, went into the bathroom, locked the door, started the shower, and then stepped into the cold water with the dog in her arms. She held it until it cooled down. She slept on the floor of the bathroom that night, beside the cool of the toilet. Kruk never came for her. She found him in bed the next day at noon, asleep and snoring.

She scooped the dead dog from the bathtub, wrapped it in towels, and carried it down to Crawfish Creek, where she let the body drop through the water to the bottom, the towels gently moving in the current. She spent the next three hours tossing large stones onto the sunken body until it was covered entirely. An underwater cairn and headstone. When she finally turned to walk back to the house, there he was, right behind her. He struck her across the head with the back of his hand. She went down, holding her mouth as it filled with blood.

"Once a month those men come out, lay their bets, pay me money to fight their dogs," he said over her, savagely. "Once a goddamn month. You never have to *see* it or even know it, okay? You can just go ahead and forget what you saw. They're just animals." He breathed quickly, put his hands on his hips, and scanned the fields as if for witnesses. Then he leaned down to her, touched her shoulder. "I'm sorry," he said. "I shouldn't have done that. But damn it, girl. I told you to stay away from the barn."

He turned away from her, striding over the desiccated cornstalks. Thereafter she could not be unafraid of him, and the dogs sensed it. She suspected him of training them against her. She kept steak in her pockets, fed them whiskey when he was away. Sang them lullabies as they lounged on the kitchen floor, drunk and full. She did love them, their big eyes and long tongues, felt safer in the house with them beside her, her protectors, their bodies warming the drafty old house through the long, quiet winter. They curled around her on the couch as she read, the heat of their bellies resting atop her cold feet.

She was afraid to run, had no friends, and nowhere to go. Most of that fall, winter, and spring they lived quietly, taking walks, cooking. A week in Corpus Christi eating fresh shrimp and crab, him having his way with her in a seaside motel to the steady soundtrack of warm, crashing surf. She'd kept her eyes shut or focused on the shifting shadows of other guests walking past their window blinds.

She was trapped, his viciousness and kindness meshed together to form their own cage. She tried steadily to separate the dog killer from the man who was her lover and companion, but the two figures constantly came together into one and it unnerved her. She did not understand killing at all. No one in her family had ever even hunted. On the nights of the fights she tried to be away, to make the whole thing disappear. Those evenings she spent driving the prairies, breaking at truck stops to pee and buy snacks, soda. She took solace in the country music played in such places at low, comforting volumes. In the mornings she found handwritten notes that he'd left on the kitchen table:

Who was I before you? Love, Bret

She called the police one day from the pet store, anonymously. Reported that there was an illegal dog-fighting syndicate operating in a barn off the Crawfish Creek. It was late spring then, and she wanted it all to come to an end. She hoped that the police would scare Bret and he would shut down the operation on his own accord. The officer on the other end of the line listened to her and kept asking her name. She repeated the information and hung up. A day later a police car rolled up their gravel road and two officers knocked on the door.

"We've got a report of some dog fighting on these premises," a woman cop had said, her long red hair flowing out from behind a brown patrol hat. She was tall and lean, her skin very pale and freckled in places.

Bethany shook her head, shrugged her shoulders. "No idea," she said. "We've got some dogs, sure. But I don't know about any fighting." She leaned on the door, her body weak.

Officer Aida Battle looked at her, removed her hat,

smoothed back that fiery hair. They had not yet met. "Ma'am, are you sure?"

Bethany nodded.

"Can we get a look at that barn?" the other officer asked, motioning with his thumb.

Bethany nodded again, unable to meet their eyes. The male officer went off toward the barn. Bethany watched him open the swinging doors and go inside. She felt the redheaded woman's eyes on her.

"I should get your name," the female cop asked. "No matter what, I ought to get your name."

"Bethany," she said. "Bethany Evers."

The male officer was already coming back. He shrugged his shoulders at the female officer, said, "I got nothing. Five or six dogs. Not uncommon on a farm like this. No other signs of anything unusual."

The redhead studied Bethany's face and then glanced toward the barn. She said, "Bethany, if you ever need to reach me for anything, here's my information. Sorry to disturb you." She handed Bethany a business card. She donned her hat again, smiled brusquely, and turned. Bethany exhaled. The female officer turned back.

"Bethany," she asked, "what do you all farm out here?"

Bethany paused, thought quickly. "There's no money in farming anymore. It's just cheap, is all. And quiet." She smiled, though her eyes pleaded with the officer. *Your partner is in on it*, she thought. *A barn full of pit bulls. He never mentioned they were pit bulls.* "The dogs like it," she said, lying. "My boyfriend inherited the land from his grandmother." She did not want them to go.

Aida nodded, kicked the dry ground, began walking away. In the distance she saw a circle of old, disturbed coals. The memory of a large fire. She walked back to the police car. Her partner was already in the car. It was unusual that she would ride with another officer and had spent most of her career patrolling alone, but her lieutenant had suggested that Lombard ride along. The address in question was in the middle of nowhere, and Officer Battle was close to retirement.

"I don't need that on my shoulders," he joked. "You go out and don't come back. So close to retirement and fruity drinks on some Floridian beach. No. Take Lombard along, guy couldn't find his ass with both hands. Show him those back roads."

They drove back down the gravel driveway and through the hulking shadow of the red barn. At the road, they met Kruk's truck. He waved happily to them, rolled down his window, and stuck an elbow out. In the bed of the truck were three pit bulls, their tongues lolling. "Hello, Officers," he said. "Can I help you?" He blocked the sun from his eyes, squinted.

Aida peered at the dogs in the bed of the truck, their nails loud on the metal. They barked incessantly. "What kind of dogs are those?" she asked.

"Terriers," he said, nodding. "Magnificent dogs."

"Pit bulls," she said, nodding back at him. "Right? Pit bulls?"

He spat at the ground, grinning. "I don't call them that, Officer. They're my pets and I love them."

"That why you've got them riding in back?" she replied. "If you loved them, you might let them ride in the cab with you. Maybe even buckle them in. Fact is, I could give you a ticket right now." She wanted to see more of his face, but it was obscured in the shadow of his visored hand.

"Aida . . ." Lombard said quietly out the side of his mouth as he pretended to peer out the passenger-side window.

"We just came from the creek," Kruk said. "They were playing. Havin' a ball. I didn't want to smell like wet dog. My girlfriend hates that." He smiled again, his teeth showing.

"Yeah, we just met her," said Aida, putting the cruiser into park. "Nice lady. Showed Officer Lombard here the barn." She tried to remember the young woman's name but couldn't. *I just met her,* Aida thought. She waited for a reaction from the man.

Kruk did not flinch, though he did rub the stubble of his face with a hand. Looking more closely at the passenger side of the police cruiser, he smiled and gave a wave. "Officer Lombard, didn't see you at first."

Lombard waved meekly back. Kruk smiled at Aida, shrugged. "It's a nice spot for dogs," he said finally. "So much freedom, you know? Room to roam."

Aida put the car back into drive, her foot on the brake. "They're dry already," she said.

"What?" asked Kruk.

"Your dogs," she said, "they're dry."

He blinked.

"You said you were up at the creek. Those dogs look dry."

Kruk looked over his shoulder at the three panting dogs. "They dry off quick in the back of the truck like that. My little secret." And then passing them on his own driveway, he gave them a wave somewhere between friendly and dismissive.

"Seems like a nice guy," Lombard said.

"Yeah, how about that? You knew him this whole time and you never let that slip. Why didn't you say something?"

Lombard spit out the window, scratched at the back of his head. "I didn't realize he lived out here, is all." He shrugged. "So I see him at the bar sometimes. What's the big deal?"

"I don't like something," Aida said. "Something ain't right."

When Bethany finished her story, Aida paused. "I remember that day, Bethany," she said. "I remember not believing him. But that's all the more reason why I still have to go after him. He's got my gun, for one thing. I can't let that go. The lieutenant will have my ass. Jesus." She could not believe she hadn't recognized the girl, hadn't recognized Kruk. *Her face, I didn't recognize her face with the scars,* she thought. *My goddamn mind is going. Unraveling.*

"You can't," Bethany said. "Not right now. Just take me to the hospital. I'll need more stitches."

Aida shook her head. "You don't get it. By all rights, I ought to have him already. Pulled over and in cuffs." She shrugged off Bethany's grip. Decades of untarnished service to lose her pistol this close to retirement; Aida was livid, scared. "I'll get backup. More cops."

"They won't care," Bethany said stiffly.

"What do you mean?" Aida said, exasperated. "What do you mean, *they won't care?*"

"They're all in on it too," Bethany said, blood everywhere, drying black. "The whole town's in on it. Your buddy in the car that day, I bet."

"Impossible," Aida said. "This is serious. Abuse of animals, gambling, racketeering."

Bethany was shaking her head. "They just think they're animals." She wiped her eyes. "I've seen it. The way they throw their dogs away afterward. Check the creek. Check the ditches. You'll see. Just walking the road near our house I've collected eighty collars. Eighty."

Aida was quiet.

"They don't care about your gun, Officer Battle," said Bethany. She reached into the pocket of her denim skirt and produced Aida's card, held it up. "All they want to do is bet money on dogs. Now, can you take me to the hospital?"

She knows my name. She has my card. "I can't do that," said Aida. "The hospital will make me file a report. I can't lie."

"Then I'll take myself," Bethany said. "Won't be the first time." She wiped the counter off, the dried spots of blood. Her manager's car was now idling in the parking lot, where he sat, eating fast food from a greasy bag. He had just pulled up.

Aida moved toward the door, stunned. She stopped in the doorway and said, "I'm sorry, Brittany. I'm sorry that I wasn't able to help you."

"It's Bethany," the young woman said, "and you forgot your dog food."

Aida waved her hand in the air, crawled into her cruiser, and felt the lightness of her belt and holster. Pulling away from the pet store, she reached for the radio to alert other cars of the assault, but then paused. She tried to remember what color the truck was that Kruk had been driving. Had it been red? Black? She pulled onto the road and drove quickly in the direction she thought he had gone, but the road led rapidly out of town and onto the prairie. Ahead of her, nothing but flat fields and trains delineating the horizon. She exited the road, driving onto a gravel track that she knew led to the train tracks. She watched a freight train rush by her patrol vehicle, the graffitied cars a blur before her. She rolled down her window and sucked in the air. *What just happened? What just happened?*

Back at the station she walked in, went to her desk, and found Lombard in her spot, on the telephone, talking to his wife.

"Took you long enough," Sergeant Doty said. "Where's the dog chow? The kibble and bits?" He scoffed, examined the box scores of a crumpled newspaper.

"What's the deal?" she asked the room. The men shrugged, rolled their eyes, kept hitting their keyboards. Lombard hung up.

"What the hell?" she asked him.

He threw his hands in the air. "What do you want, Battle?" he asked. "You forget where your damn desk is?" The men in the office liked to tease her about her memory. She was always losing things: her hat, reports, her coffee mug. They said she was getting old.

"My desk," she said.

"This is my desk," he said.

She opened the top right drawer, where she stored a package of tampons, though she was past the age of needing them. They were not there. She reached across his crotch to the top left drawer, where she kept two packages of Dixon Ticonderoga No. 2 pencils, all deftly sharpened. The drawer was a tangle of rubber bands over a layer of glossy fantasy football magazines.

"Hey!" Lombard said. "Quit snooping! That's my shit!" He slammed the drawer shut.

She stormed out of the office and the men roared with laughter. In the locker room she splashed cold water on her face, let her hair fall loose, breathed deeply. She went to her locker and opened it to an avalanche of Titleist golf balls, all bouncing around the room loudly. She was startled, confused, her mind reeling. *Did I leave that young girl back there? Why didn't I help her? Why didn't I recognize her or that man?*

Just then her colleagues came into the locker room, a sheet cake in the lieutenant's hands ablaze with candles. They sang loudly to her, "Auld Lang Syne" and "For She's a Jolly Good Fellow," bottles of beer already open in their thick hands. She smiled, beaten and confused, and holding back her own hair, blew out the candles as she was expected to.

"We'll miss you," the lieutenant said, his hand on her shoulder.

"I guess you didn't even need the dog food," she said over him to the K9 unit. They grinned like wolves.

"One other thing," she said to the lieutenant later in the evening, pulling him close and whispering, "I lost my pistol. Twenty-five years on patrol, and I lose my pistol going to the pet store on a prank." She shook her head. "How much paperwork does that earn me?"

"Don't worry about it," he said. "Eat your cake. In a few months you won't need it anyway." Then, "Lord, Aida. That memory of yours. Must be some rust on that steel trap of yours, huh?"

She shook her head.

She ate the cake and drank beer with the other highway patrolmen. Then, protocol be damned, they broke into a box of cigars and the room began to fill with thick, dank smoke. Her eyes reddened as she looked over the room and wondered which among these men took their thrills from watching the slaughter of dogs. There was a fog accumulating inside her head and it frightened her. She had become a cop to protect people, but lately . . . she was weak, easily duped, so confused. Her memory failing her.

Driving home that evening early, she narrowly missed several deer on the roads. Inside her house she made a mug of instant coffee, stirring the fine particles of coffee into the boiling water. Within the useless chicken wire of her garden, two fawns were chewing on her lettuce plants and she saw rabbits among the radishes and carrot tops. She had misgivings about retirement. She knew she needed to see a doctor, but was afraid of the notion of a brain scan, scared to think of her body entering the pounding tube of a CAT scan. She feared Alzheimer's even more. She lived alone and wondered if her isolation was responsible for the broken connections inside her head. She was always forgetting things, many things. Everything. Not long ago she'd left the prowler in her driveway overnight, idling, lights on, until the gas tank ran empty. The next morning she had to pour a gallon of gasoline from a jerry can into the tank, gas meant for the lawn mower but enough to get her back into town. Other things too: She had forgotten the lieutenant's name, had handed a speeding ticket to a waitress instead of her money, wore tennis shoes to work three mornings in a row. It was Lombard who gently pointed to her feet.

She thought of Bethany and realized in that moment at her kitchen sink, looking out into the growing shadows of the gloaming, that the reason why the young woman had not pressed her to arrest the man was that she wanted him killed or dealt with in different terms. And what good could possibly come from involving the police, the same men she knew were complicit in his crimes? And then just as suddenly, Aida recognized the scars on her face. They were not from any kind of blade. They were the scars of a face bitten by a dog, maybe many dogs. The kind of scar she saw most frequently on the dirty faces of neglected young children.

She moved into her den, set a record on the turntable, poured a glass of bourbon, and listened to Dave Brubeck for several hours, unnerved and ashamed. Over and over she listened to that record, flipping it almost like a pancake every time the needle signaled her to do so, as if hypnotized. Bethany was all alone in the world. Twice she had failed to help the woman. Inside her lonely house, Aida felt like an inadequate guardian. She felt afraid, cradled the bourbon, and ran her fingers through her hair. Then some time in the middle of the night, with coyotes sounding out in the fields beyond her windows, she listened to the record wobble as it spun without music, the needle swimming out over the record's dark and grooveless center. She sat that way until dawn, blurry. The turntable scratching, the needle a single claw.

Bethany called from the pet store one week into Aida's retirement. She wanted to meet somewhere discreet. She had been living at a roadside motel for several months, her money now almost gone. There had been hail forecast for that day, tornadoes sighted already in western counties.

She told Aida then how the dogs had taken her face, how she escaped the farm, how she could not quit her job because she needed the money, how her manager could no longer look her in the eyes, how the procedure to save her face had amounted now to a mountain of debt that she knew she could not pay off. How the pain of her stitched-together visage made it impossible to sleep on a bed, her face on a pillow. How she slept in chairs at night and dreamed of dead dogs and teeth wrapping around her skull, like a softball.

They met the next day at the café beside the highway. That morning Aida had gone to a gun show in Red Wing and bought a new pistol in order to reclaim her old one. Aida had pieced together Bethany's situation on a legal pad; she had taken notes with a pencil. Kept underlining: BETHANY, PIT BULLS, BARN, FACE. She underlined BETHANY until the graphite broke, ripped a jagged hole right through the paper. Fingering the hole where the name had just been, she could no longer remember what had been there. "Started with a B," she said, "started with a B."

They came to the barn on the first night of every new moon, when the night was entirely black and the animals less susceptible to the moon's weird whims. The barn held about two hundred people packed in tight, elbow to elbow, belt buckle to belt buckle, most of them parking their asses on a set of old wooden bleachers Kruk had bought from a high school remodeling their gymnasium.

Aida watched as her old colleagues came through the barn doors, already drunk, carrying handles of cheap liquor, their fists full of fragrant cigars. Then the parade of politicians, schoolteachers, attorneys, and businessmen. Kruk greeted them all at the door, writing their bets in a book, and taking their money.

The newcomers came up the driveway with their headlights blazing, the veterans navigated in darkness, the stars overhead crisp and clearly visible and the two tracks of the driveway familiar. She watched them file into the barn from her vantage in the farmhouse, the metal of the pistol cold and real against the pale skin of her lower back where the muzzle nestled beneath the elastic of her panties. The night was alive with dogs.

Most of the fights lasted only minutes; she could construct in her head the inside of the barn through the cheers and jeers of the men assembled: the initial prefight rumblings, then the off-leash fervor, the tenacious encouragements and insults, and finally the agonized pleadings and overjoyed exclamations. The sound of money changing hands was there too, in the night air, like the quaking of old aspen leaves. In between fights she spied the men leaving the barn, pissing into the darkness, the cherries of their cigarettes and cigars briefly illuminating their drunk faces. She watched as some owners carried their dogs out of the barn like dead children, kissing them. Others kicked the dying creatures and carcasses out into the near night, the light of the barn in their fading eyes. She watched a man piss on a beaten, bleating dog. At times it was difficult to separate the sounds of men from those of the dogs. Worst was the sound of stomping boots on the wooden bleachers. It caused the hair to stand up on her neck.

She whispered to herself, "Stay together now, girl."

The final match lasted what must have been an hour, the voices of the men growing low and hoarse with the protracted battle. She watched the spectators emerge into the night, vomiting, their hands on the sides of the barn. Others left, their tires spinning gravel into the air.

"He's fighting blind," she heard one man say. "Got no eyes left."

The match ended near dawn, the sky bruising blue and yellow. The men left, some with their dogs. She went into the closet beside the old mattress and shut the folding doors, waited for him to come up the stairs, his boots heavy. She tried to breathe evenly. Downstairs, a door opened. She waited for the sounds of canine claws on the old wood, but there was nothing, just the noise of a bottle being extracted from the refrigerator, a cap popped off. She would have been found by now if there had been dogs, would've had to act first. She sighed in relief. Finally he came up.

He removed his shirt, his back and chest marred with crude tattoos. He sat heavily on the bed, yawned, scratched at his whiskers, and slowly pulled off his boots and socks. He was asleep inside a minute. She eased the folding doors open, the gun already drawn, then moved across the room, aiming for his face. He snored, his lips moving. She stood beside him, so close that she could smell the sweat and blood on him. Then she whipped him with the pistol across the face, gouged the bridge of his nose. He sucked air and howled. She edged back. Outside, dogs barked inside a dark barn.

"On your feet," she said, taking a half step backward.

He looked at her, smiled. "I thought you were retired." Moving his neck forward, he spat blood at her boots. "Surprised you remembered how to get out here . . ."

She fired a bullet at the floor, the room suddenly smelling of gunpowder and smoke, her ears ringing with the blast. "Don't fuck with me," she said. "On the floor." She indicated with the smoking barrel of her pistol.

He crept to the floor and lay down, eyes never leaving her. She handcuffed him, grabbed his hair, and slammed his face into the wood.

"You got it right this time!" he said. "What is it? Alzheimer's? I see it, you know. See it in your eyes. They're all glassy. You're losing it more and more, ain't you?"

"What happened to her?" she asked, shaking her head. High on adrenaline and at the same time oddly drowsy, she felt wobbly. It was still dark in the room, just the ambient light of the stars.

"I told her not to show fear," he said. "She couldn't do it. She wasn't strong enough. They'll smell it on a person. I smell it on you."

"We'll go for a walk," she said. "You can tell me then."

They walked out of the house, over the field toward the creek. He tripped on the cornstalks, falling down. "Look, lady, I don't know what happened," he said. "Best bet is, she didn't realize they'd come into the house after a fight. Maybe their muzzles were torn open. Maybe they were raw, angry. I expect she tripped over them in the night, on her way to the bathroom. Honestly, I don't know. I mean, I dropped her off outside the hospital." He shrugged. "I told her not to be afraid. Where'd she go anyway? Haven't seen her face in a while. Not since I stole your gun. You remember that, don't you?"

Aida whipped him again. They were close to the creek. She heard the sucking and whoosh of the water around tree roots and fallen trunks. He stopped at the bank. In the water she saw a strange pyramid of rocks. "Get in there," she said.

"The hell I will," he said. "I'll drown."

"Get."

He stumbled into the water but kept his footing. Never broke down, never wept or begged. He stood in the middle of the narrow creek, arms behind him, blood trickling into his mouth.

"Where's the money?" she asked.

He spat into the creek and the blood went away.

"Last chance," she said, pulling the hammer back.

"In the freezer," he said. "Some more underneath a floorboard up in my bedroom."

"How much?"

"I don't know," he said. "You count it."

She shot him twice then, and his body spun backward into the creek. She watched him drift away until his body became entangled in an old fence line cutting through the creek along with all the other debris: ragged plastic bags, branches, cornstalks. She watched as the water broke against him, pushing him farther down into the murk. Then she went back to the house.

Inside, she stacked the money from the freezer on the kitchen table. It was rubber-banded into thick wads and wrapped in Saran. Her old service piece was in the freezer too, next to Ziploc bags full of rhubarb, sweet corn, and tomatoes. And a deed to the house, signed over to him by an Ione Miller. She set these things on the table and went upstairs.

She opened the folding doors and the mattress fell down onto the floor. Only the way it fell did not sound right. A single hundred-dollar bill floated through the air, falling to the floor like an expired leaf. She looked at the mattress more closely. There was an incision in the side and she saw that the mattress was stuffed with cash, bonds. *This money wasn't his*, Aida thought. The dates on some of the bills were from the 1920s. She counted the cash as she extracted it from the musty old pad. Ninety thousand dollars. In the closet, beneath a floorboard, fifty thousand more. She went down the stairs with the money heaped in her arms, stuffed into pillowcases. She carried everything out to her truck, looking over her shoulder toward the field and the creek. There was barking inside the barn. She locked the doors to the truck and moved toward the giant red building. Dawn had come.

Inside, one dog yet barely alive, entrails hanging from

his belly to the dirty floor, and chained to an old cow stanchion trembling with fear. Aida came to it, her hands on its sides gently. She freed the dog, but it only leaned into her. She carried it back to the truck, its eyes searching. She drove down the driveway, her eyes on the rearview mirror. She looked back at the gravel path before her. An Escalade had just turned into the driveway and was moving toward her. It pulled to the shoulder, and she saw the driver roll down his window. She recognized him as a pharmacist. Saw his breath in the early morning cool.

"Officer Battle," he said, looking embarrassed. He saw the dog beside her in the truck, the pile of money. "Didn't know you fought dogs."

"Wilson," she said, "you have any morphine on you?" His name came effortlessly, from some fathoms deep inside her. She let the words come up.

He startled. "He in bad shape?"

She fingered the pistol beside her, was irate inside. "He's damn near gone," she said.

"Don't waste the drugs," he said, waving his hand. "Bullets are cheaper."

"That right?" she said.

She pulled the pistol out, leveled her wrist on the window frame, and put two bullets in each of his driver-side tires. The dog startled, shook. Wilson stared at her. "Morphine," she said.

He rode in the bed of the truck to the veterinarian's office. She made him carry the dog in himself.

"You fight another dog," she told him, "I'll do more than ruin your vehicle."

He nodded, walking into the back of the building with the wounded animal.

She went back to her house, pulling the F-150 into her driveway. Blood on the bench seat and a bag of money. She folded out of the truck, every nerve inside her body bent and charged. Just then two fawns burst out of her browned garden and she pulled the pistol from the small of her back and aimed at them, but they'd already bounded into the safety of a nearby copse of birch. She tried the front door, but it was locked. The keys in her hands jingled together and it was difficult for her to fit the metal inside the lock. Pushing against the door, she began sobbing. She was breaking and there was no one for her. Finally the door gave way and she allowed herself to lay right down in the doorway. She had the sudden desire to own a dog, a pet, some kind creature to comfort her. She fell asleep that way and lay there until the afternoon sun was hot enough to induce sweat. Then picked herself up and went inside, closing the door. Leaves had collected in the threshold.

The answering machine was blinking on the kitchen counter and she went to it, pressed the button. It was the lieutenant. "Battle. It's LT. Look, got a strange report of Doctor Wilson showing up at the vet's office holding a dead dog. Said you'd dropped him there? Said he had two flats out by that farmhouse you and Lombard visited. You remember . . ." But the tape had run out, his voice stopping abruptly. The machine said, "Message two." It was the lieutenant's voice again. "Damn machines. Look, I know you're retired and everything, Battle, but I need you to call me on this one, all right? I sent Lombard out there this morning to check on things and no one was home. That kid Kruk might be mixed up in something and he wasn't around, though his red Dodge truck was. So if . . ." The machine cut the lieutenant's voice off again and then said, "You have no more messages."

It was red, she thought, *how could I have forgotten a red Ram? A red Ram. A red goddamn Ram.*

She reached into the cupboard for a coffee mug, staring out the window the whole time. The driver-side door of the truck was open. She filled the kettle with water and put it on the stove to boil. She went outside to the truck where the money was still on the seat. She eased into the truck and tried to turn on the radio but did not have her keys. She went into the house and found the keys beside the answering machine, looked out the window. The truck door was still open. She went outside and then sat on the bench seat again, turning the keys in the ignition. The radio warbled on and she sat that way for some time, listening to country music until night set in. Inside the house, a whistle was blowing and the kitchen windows were foggy with steam. The stovetop was everywhere wet with water that had sputtered out of the kettle. *What was I doing? What a mess. What a mess.* On the kitchen table was a bag full of money.

In Duluth, Aida found Bethany beside the great lake, watching freighters go slowly by. It was the first day of November, and Bethany had a cashmere scarf knotted around her face.

"It's the only thing that can touch my face," she said. "So goddamned expensive, but it's the only thing that feels good."

They sat on the gray, weathered seat of a park bench. Aida kicked a duffel bag toward Bethany's right shoe.

"I'm not dumb, you know," Bethany said after a while. "I want you to know that. You probably think I am . . . but I'm not. I went to college. I was just no good with men. Could never say the right thing, so . . . I just stopped talking. I thought I'd won the lottery with Bret. You should have seen him with those dogs sometimes." She wiped her nose with the back of her hand gently. "Especially in the mornings. They'd hop up onto the bed and be licking at his face and I can hear his laughter." She threw a stone into the lake. She thought about him again and shivered uneasily. He had not been a good man; he had duped her. She unzipped the duffel bag, tilted her head.

"Should be enough for whatever surgery you need," Aida said. Then "I took fifty already. That number seemed about right. Too bad about that house, though. Who knows if she had any kin. Seemed like a nice enough place there, near the creek and all."

"No," Bethany said, "I hope it gets burnt to the ground. All of it." Then, "You didn't remember me at all, did you?"

She moved her fingers lightly over the scars on her face. "Are they that bad? The scars?"

Aida shook her head, her teeth cold in the wind. "I got an appointment at the Mayo hospital down in Rochester, but I don't even know if I can stand to go. Don't know if I care to hear the bad news." She paused. The air smelled fresh, a suggestion of snow not too far away, but also of other things: diesel, fish, sawdust. "No," she said, "they aren't that bad. But no. I didn't recognize you. Not even sure I filed a report for that day. If I think back to it, I can't even remember driving back to the station that day. Just . . . whole days gone. Whole days."

"I'll go with you," Bethany said, looking at Aida. But Aida never acknowledged the words and maybe the wind had come across the lake and swooped them up because the redheaded woman sat still, regarding the expanse of water ahead of her. Her lips moving very minutely and Bethany realized that she was talking to herself as if no one else was around. *Whole days, whole days.*

They sat together, the wind sweeping their hair into their faces. Out on the lake the freighters moved slowly and white-caps were building, crashing against the piers and riprap. Above them, abandoned grain elevators rose into the blue sky and pigeons circled. They watched a three-legged dog trot through a field of rusted trucks, its black nose in the air, sniffing the freshwater breezes.

TRAIN PEOPLE MOVE SLOW

THE PYRAMIDS OF BURNING LEAVES smoldered into the night, even with the rain, and inside our house and on our clothes the smoke clung like gray cologne, and it was easy to know that it was November. That night, under the porch, Sunny found the cat, emaciated, its fur matted with shit. We had heard a noise all night long, and at first I'd thought it was just mice in the walls, but then both of us got out of bed and started tracking the noise until finally Sunny found it, its meow loud, plaintive, persistent.

Hearing our movements in the night, the girls woke up and tumbled after each other down the stairs. The last rust-colored leaves were being knocked off the black fingers of the trees by the rain. I remember thinking it seemed too early for snow but that maybe it would. It made me cold to see Sunny outside in her old high school volleyball shorts, her legs naked, toenails immaculately painted, her narrow back bent down beneath the porch as she cooed to the bedraggled creature.

"What is it, Mom?" the girls asked nearly in unison. They were under my arms, wrapped around me. I'd never wanted kids, but the girls had come with Sunny and now they were mine. Two little girls with hair blacker than their mother's. We lived near the river, where fishermen caught giant carp and catfish and sometimes even sturgeon below the drain-pipes of the paper company, where the river never froze. I looked across the river at the plant, where steam rose up into the falling rain and held the lights of industry, making the entire complex glow like a ghost ship in the night.

"It's a cat," Sunny said. The girls trilled behind their tiny fingers.

"Baby," I said, "get back in the house, it's freezing."

"All the more reason to bring this cat inside," she responded. Her voice was sharp.

I never argued with Sunny. She'd had a hard life before, and I wanted her life with me to be easy. There were times she pushed me around, times she even gave me black eyes, but it was worth it. Everything was better with Sunny. Even when she was casting flour around the kitchen or acciden-tally setting the drapes on fire. Being in love with Sunny was like that; it was like a fistfight. She entered every relation-ship with brass knuckles, and I had a glass jaw for love. I was willing to be beaten down for those evenings when she crawled back into bed after the bars, her face against my chest, her hair all cigarette smoke, her voice raw and throaty.

"I love you," she always said. "You should leave us, you know? Do yourself a favor and leave us."

But I never said anything. It was better to just be quiet and to let things mellow, my fingers combing her hair in the red glow of the clock radio. Sunny was the best lover I'd ever had. Some nights we took the mattress off the bed frame and made love on the floor, where it was more quiet, my fingers in her mouth to keep her mute, her teeth digging into me and making marks.

Sunny finally grabbed the cat by its scruff and held it up into the corona of the porch light. The creature could not have weighed five pounds.

"I'll get a bowl of milk," said Nina.

"Warm it up!" yelled her younger sister, Char. The girls ran off toward the kitchen and there was the sound of dishes crashing to the floor.

"I'm allergic to cats," I said to Sunny, but she just kissed me, her lips wet with the rain.

"Benadryl," she said, patting my stomach gently and then letting her hand run down a little lower.

She walked into the house with the cat, and following her, I closed the door on the night. My shift at the paper plant started in less than five hours, and the three women in my life were all screaming with delight as they bathed the putrid feline in the kitchen sink. From the entryway I could see spilled milk and broken china on the kitchen's linoleum floor. I made a mental note to clean it up when I awoke in the morning.

I had met Sunny almost exactly a year earlier, in November. I was down by the river, fishing with the old Hmong men and the old black men, all of us hunched over on plastic pickle buckets, all of us looking out over the swirling eddies, waiting for something to happen. I had always been a bachelor; I didn't know how to meet women, not really. I'd had lovers in college, but it was always almost accidental, those magnetic couplings wrought out of beer and pot, intimacies that by morning had come undone, unbound, and sometimes we'd drive to a truck stop or a café for breakfast, but frequently not, and the girls would simply collect their clothes in a ball and leave without a word.

The fishing had been steady that day, and I had just hooked a pretty good-sized carp when a car slammed on its brakes at the top of the riverbank. Reeling hard, I glanced over my shoulder and saw a figure pushed out of the automobile, an old Hornet, just as it sped off, its open passenger door clapping shut. None of the other fishermen seemed to notice. I hesitated before cutting the line, but it was the only thing to do. I scrambled up the talus of the bank in my old Wellingtons, out of breath.

She was lying down on the asphalt, knees up in the air, boots on the pavement, her hair arrayed around her head like a black halo. One arm was flat on the ground, the other moving a cigarette toward her lips. She had a cut on her forehead, not big, the blood already coagulating in the cold.

"You all right?" I asked.

She didn't answer right away, and if she hadn't been smoking, I might have kicked her softly with a boot to see if she was alive. Behind me, the river moved huge and slow, one great broad brown stroke of movement and sound, and beyond it I heard a whistle from the paper plant and the beeping sound of a forklift in reverse. I moved closer to her and extended my hand. She was crying, I saw now, only without making any noise.

"Get up," I said, and it was the only order I ever gave Sunny. She took my hand and struggled up. I handed her a red handkerchief, which she used to wipe her face and nose. Then she stuck the cloth in her pocket as if it were her own, something she'd just happened to find. On the handkerchief were my initials, stitched there by my grandmother, now gone.

"Want something to drink?" I asked.

She nodded her head and we moved back down to the river. I helped her navigate the talus, and when we reached the shore I motioned to my pickle bucket. She sat and crossed her muscular legs. They were the legs of a gymnast or a volleyball player, thick and shapely. She flicked the last of her cigarette into the water, and I watched the filter do pirouettes in the water until a carp rose and made it disappear into the murk.

"Did you see that?" she said. There was excitement in her voice as she pointed to the disappearance.

"They'll eat anything," I said.

"It ate my *cigarette*," she said, delighted. "It ate my fucking cigarette." Then: "I wonder if it was still burning a little."

I unscrewed my thermos and poured her a cup of coffee. She reached for it through the cold air and I could see that her fingers were long and beautiful and trembling slightly with what I thought was the cold. There were many rings on her fingers and her nails were painted a color between black and purple.

"My name is Bruce," I said.

"Sunny," she answered, shifting the coffee from one hand to the other as she shook my hand. Her grip was strong.

"Got any milk?" she asked. "Sugar? Brandy?"

"I have this," I said, and reached into a pocket of my vest, producing a silver flask that my best friend had given me many years before, just after high school, when we were still in touch.

Sunny unscrewed the top and sniffed.

"Bulleit?" she asked.

I raised an eyebrow. "It's my favorite."

I didn't know then that Sunny was an alcoholic, and later there were times I wished I had known, because early on, we would sit together by the river, drinking Bulleit or sometimes splitting thirty cans of Hamm's, and I would think how she drank faster than anyone I'd ever seen, as if she were drowning but couldn't help herself and kept gulping down the burn until it almost shut her faculties off, until she would either pass out or go about the world like an angry zombie and sometimes I could escort her home without incident, but there were more nights when she would start swearing at me in the street or in a bar or even on the front lawn, the girls' faces pressed to the front windows and a skittish babysitter behind them, a telephone in her hands.

"One of mine too," she said, taking a pull off the flask and then pouring more than a few thimbles into her coffee.

I began tying a new leader to the line, then clamped a new lead weight on the line and selected a big, bright lure. It made me happy to have company, and when I looked down the shore, the Hmong men and the black men were smiling at me, their faces shiny and happy, their own flasks and Styrofoam cups raised in a quick toast.

"I like it down here," Sunny said. "It's peaceful. Except for that paper plant over there." She motioned to the long complex of buildings and stacks, then sipped her coffee.

"I work over there," I said.

"Oh," Sunny said. "Sorry."

"That's all right," I said. "Not exactly a glamorous job."

Sunny smiled out over the water and then I felt her eyes on me, even though I was concentrating on a knot and attempting to look my most rugged and trying to ignore her just enough to let her know I was interested. The thing was, I didn't know what to do with my own eyes, and when I finished the knot I took a chance and looked at her, right in the eyes, and that was the first time I recognized how beautiful she was and she swept some of her long black hair away from her face and I could see that she wore big silver hoop earrings and that I was in love, all of a sudden. And I knew it, could feel it, right in my heart. She looked right back at me.

"Want to get out of here?" she asked.

I packed up my tackle box and rod and almost forgot my thermos until the other fisherman saw me working my way up the bank and yelled and started laughing, pointing to the thermos sitting right there atop the pickle bucket, big as an artillery shell.

Sunny moved in a month later, and the girls came with her, and all of a sudden my house felt like a new dwelling, warm and loud and full of the smells of women: soap, perfume, hair spray. Sunny smoked, but it was all right because mostly she stood on the front porch and watched the river through the naked trees, but sometimes she kept an ashtray beside our bed, and after we made love she would set the ashtray on her flat brown stomach and smoke and I would have to open a window, even in winter. She always tried to get me to smoke too, but I'd never liked anything other than White Owls or Swishers, and this made her laugh.

"First man I ever had who didn't smoke," she said, shaking her head. "Who am I gonna bum 'em from now?"

Sometimes Sunny said things like that—things that were supposed to sound funny but just came out crass or ugly. I never talked to her about the women I'd been with, and I didn't like to imagine her with her past lovers, lying in bed together and sharing a single cigarette because it was an intimate thing and something I knew we would never share.

Sunny never worked and I never asked her where the

money she had came from. She didn't have much most of the time, but then suddenly she would, and she would come home from the grocery store and suddenly our cupboards would be full and the girls would be eating their favorite sugary cereals. Once I came home from the plant to discover four huge lobsters boiling in a pot and a bottle of champagne in a snowbank beside the front porch.

"You win the lottery?" I asked.

"Maybe," she said, wrapping her arms around my waist and kissing me, the taste of drawn butter already on her mouth.

"Seriously," I asked.

"Seriously!" She pantomimed.

"We found it," she crowed, "didn't we, girls? In a briefcase down by the river."

The girls nodded, as if previously coached, and continued their crunching. I kissed them both and hung up my coat on the rack. Then picked up three other coats off the floor and hung them up too.

"You *found* the money for lobsters and champagne and all that other stuff."

Sunny nodded her head and crossed her muscular legs. She liked to wear shorts in the house, no matter the weather outside, and she knew this discombobulated me. I could see that her legs were freshly shaved and she had changed the polish on her toenails. The house felt warm and I checked the thermostat.

"Eighty!" I cried.

The girls laughed, and so did Sunny. I could see that Sunny was drinking mimosas, and I wondered if there was already an empty bottle of champagne somewhere out in the backyard, wedged into the snow.

But then we ate dinner together, the girls laughing and heckling me and Sunny running her foot up my thigh under the table and our bellies full of opulence, and like always, I let it go, the idea that maybe Sunny was running marijuana or meth, or that she'd been out to the casino while the girls were in school. I didn't want to be alone again—that much I knew.

And after we put the girls to sleep, Sunny slid a tape into the old cassette player near my bed and we would listen to Annie Ross while we made love, our bodies warm in the second story of the old house, the champagne turning us into two bubbles floating over the frozen world, and the paper plant across the river glowing through the window blinds nothing more than a chimera I could wish away while Sunny swayed over me like a sexy cobra, holding me in her trance.

Sunny didn't like my neighbors and my neighbors didn't like Sunny. Maybe they didn't like her because she was a new face, an outsider to the neighborhood, or maybe because my once-quiet bachelor pad had grown so loud and bright. Maybe they didn't like her because once a month the cops were called to our house because Sunny was playing Bon Jovi or Poison too loud. Or maybe they just didn't like her because she was so beautiful and they were jealous. I could imagine the possibilities, and yet Sunny was a mother to two beautiful girls and she was just as likely to bake someone brownies as she was to wake them in the middle of the night.

The thing was, I left for work before the sun even rose and wasn't home usually until dusk, pedaling my old Schwinn over the iron bridge and waving to the Hmong fishermen below me. So I wasn't around if there was drama during the day. The only thing I ever heard was Sunny's complaints.

"Crackheads!" she'd roar. "And meth addicts. You ever see those two bitches?" she'd ask.

"The sisters?" I'd say. "They don't bother anyone."

The sisters lived across the street from us, their backyard sloping all the way down into the river. They were in their fifties probably, and had inherited the house from their mother, who passed on just a few years after I had bought my house. The mother had been a kind old woman, and I'd shoveled her driveway and mowed her lawn sometimes. One Christmas she knit me a pair of mittens two sizes too small. I'd never met her daughters, though. They kept the house dark and rarely ever seemed to leave.

"*That's* who you have to watch," Sunny would say. "The fucking quiet ones. I'll bet you five cartons of cigarettes they're running a lab out of their basement. I'm telling you, next time you see those bitches, take a good look at their teeth and their eyes. Those women are high as kites. Trust me."

"How would you know?" I'd ask. When I came home from work I always wanted an inch of Bulleit or maybe a cold can of Hamm's, but with Sunny I had to watch these things. I dipped my hand into the refrigerator and grabbed a Coke.

"Never mind," Sunny would say, eyeing me viciously. She knew I wanted something to drink. Sunny could be mean. She liked to fight, liked to raise her voice to see what would happen. "You can't even *say* it, can you? You think I'm an addict too. Coming home nights and drinking your Coke. Don't tell me you can't taste that bourbon right now. A working stiff coming home and drinking Coke? How old are you? Sixteeen? Come on! Where's the Bulleit? Let's get it. So nice—mixin' in with that sugar in your Coke? Let's make us some! How 'bout?"

I shook my head.

"What happened with the sisters anyway?" I redirected.

Sunny grabbed the cat off the linoleum floor and began stroking his fur, the coat by now thick and lustrous.

"Geronimo was over there today," Sunny said. "And I'm telling you, I saw those bitches giving him milk."

"That doesn't sound too bad."

"Wake up!" she snapped. "They want to steal him!"

"Nobody wants to steal Geronimo," I said calmly. My eyes watered when the cat was close. Sunny waved him in my face like a weapon.

"You never wanted him anyway," she said. "Poor old kitty."

Sunny put Geronimo down and there was anger in her face. "I'm going out," she declared.

"Where?" I asked.

"I don't know," she said, nibbling her fingers, her eyes suddenly skittish and alive.

"What about the girls?" I asked, though guilt never worked with Sunny.

"I don't know. Make some macaroni and cheese. Or hot dogs. I just need to get out—you know, breathe a little."

"You want to take a walk?" I suggested.

But such lame niceties rarely merited even a sarcastic reply. She headed upstairs, and suddenly there was a spring to her movements. I watched those thighs propel her up, that butt. I could not stay angry at Sunny.

We had many nights like that. Me and the girls at the table, eating something out of a box. They talked to me about school, and sometimes we sat on the couch together afterward, both of them leaning into me as the blue light of the television washed over our faces. We made popcorn together, and the truth was, in those moments, as much as I loved Sunny, I loved the girls more. Maybe because there weren't those same lows, when I felt confused or hurt or jealous, and after I put the girls to bed I would move a rocking chair to the front porch and smoke a White Owl in the darkness and watch the river, knowing that the first green shoots of spring were popping out of the earth, that the river was swollen and huge, the banks being eaten away all the time and carried into the water and away from us—south, I suppose. I liked to imagine the bottom of the river and all the things slowly rolling on toward New Orleans and then all the way out into the Gulf of Mexico. Ancient Studebakers, old televisions, skeletons maybe, and all the debris from the paper plant that I knew was down there: pallets and metal drums and all the detritus of industry.

Sunny would come home and sometimes I would be awake, silently fuming in my porch chair. Other times the sound of an approaching motorcycle would wake me and I would flick the remains of my White Owl out into the yard and sit up in time to watch Sunny dismount the bike and nod toward the biker, always a different stranger, and then he would plow on into the night, just a red light behind him, and I would never see him again. Each time I wondered who he might be, if I could trust him or not, always in that moment focusing on him, not on Sunny as she teetered toward me, her face glazed and beaming, the orange glow of a cigarette illuminating her sparkling eyes, misty with the sadness that always shadowed her moments of joy. She would sit in my lap and look at me in the darkness and I did not know how to tell her how I felt because I was always afraid the man on the motorcycle would come back, idling his machine in front of our house.

"Such a sweet guy, you are," Sunny would say, peering at me sadly. "Why do you stay around?"

And then she would rest her head against my chest, holding her cigarette off away from me, still there and glowing.

"I love you" was all I could ever say. "I love you." And on those nights, when I told her I loved her, saying the words almost hurt because they were so true and big, and I believed in them as much as I believed in the river. But I did not believe Sunny. I did not believe, for instance, that she really heard me, so that most of the time when I told her I loved her it was like talking to someone who had died that you badly missed, someone you wanted to confide in still, but who was gone from the world, except for your memory or idea of them, haunting you like a ghost.

After such nights, things would go quiet for a while. Sunny would stay home and help the girls with their homework. The house would be clean, and sometimes when I came home from my work on my ten-speed, I would see Sunny on the front porch, smoking a cigarette, a nonalcoholic beer in her hand and a can of Hamm's ready and cold for me. We would kiss and I would sit beside her, happy to be outside, the river low in the summertime and obscured slightly by a new blind of leaves, the paper plant happily out of sight, just the smell of it in the thick, warm air.

"I'm taking a break," she would say. "I'm sorry about the other night."

Happy to have her back, I wouldn't say a word.

"I wish . . . ," she began quietly on one of those nights, "I wish sometimes you'd tell me what to do. You know? I wish you'd tell me to stop."

"I don't want to tell you anything," I said.

"I know it. But maybe you should. Like that time you told me to get up."

I was surprised, in a way, that she remembered that, the first time we met.

"You didn't think I remembered," she said, taking a drag

of her cigarette and then offering me a puff, as she always did. "I remember. I remember that creep pushing me out of his car and then laying there, thinking, 'The fuck is wrong with me? Why do I *do* this to myself?' And then you were right there and you said, 'Get up,' like some hard-ass angel or something. And I remember that fish eating my cigarette and the coffee and you know, that afternoon, making love and how your hands still smelled like the river. I remember how at first I didn't like that, but then I *did* and I liked how you had quit your fishing just for me."

She looked at me.

The thing is, most people in the world are like me, boring. But then sometimes you meet someone like Sunny, and you forgive them for being crazy or whatever, because if there weren't women like Sunny, everything would be like how my life was before her. And there would be no lobster dinners financed with magic. No beautiful daughters. No making love to jazz or making love before work and all day having her scents on me like a perfume that I could smell and be happy for.

"It was a Hornet," I said.

She looked bewildered.

"That creep, he drove a Hornet."

She shook her head at me and kissed me, and as much as I loved her, there were times I hated to taste her cigarettes, but that was Sunny's taste too, and I did love her so much.

———

In mid-August, when the river was at its lowest, we took the girls down to swim. The house was stifling, and without air conditioning we were all sleeping down in the basement where it was cool. Sometimes we pretended that it was a camping trip and lighted candles, and Sunny and I would take turns reading scary stories until the girls finally fell asleep, their skinny little bodies close to us.

The river in August was not the river in November or April. It was all sandbars and islands of gravel, junked cars visible here and there and old I beams laying around like pickup sticks from some other, more brutal time. The girls ran in and out of the water while Sunny lay on a blanket rubbing olive oil on her skin, her tan growing darker and darker, and sometimes when I glanced over at her through my sunglasses she would smile and pull her bikini bottom down a bit, where her skin was nearly as white as mine, and she would run her fingernails over her legs, and in this way I would frequently spear myself with a fishing lure or drop the rod into the river.

The fishing was not good, but I had never been much for reading, so I enjoyed the lazy work of casting into the shallow pools. It was good to concentrate on the river, watching for riffles and movements of things unseen below the surface of the water.

The largest common carp ever caught in Wisconsin was measured at over fifty-seven pounds. The fish I caught that afternoon in August was not far behind. Huge and hideously ugly, it slammed my jig and immediately began running away from the gravel bar where I stood and out into the main channel of the river. Sunny let out a hoot and jumped up, and the girls forgot their frolicking and everyone stood around me, a tiny crowd cheering me on as I reeled the behemoth in, careful not to break the line and trying to play things calmly, as if fifty-pound carp was commonplace in my own angling annals. When I finally managed to beach the monster, I sat down heavily in the gravel, sweat pouring off my face. The girls circled the fish, nearly as big as they were, tentatively poking at its huge scales with the longest sticks they could locate on short notice.

"You think I'm cooking *that* thing," said Sunny "you're crazy." Her hands were crossed over her chest.

"The carp is the largest member of the minnow family," I told her, out of breath.

"Bullshit," she said.

"I'm too tired to bullshit," I said. "It's true. That's basically a gigantic minnow."

"Daddy," said Char, "you're a good fisherman."

Sunny and Nina looked at the little girl who had just called me her father. Already buzzed from the battle with the carp, my body felt suddenly electric, invincible. Someone in the world, this little girl, thought I was her father, her dad. For the first time in my life I felt bigger than the person I was really, someone strong and worthy and heroic, and it is true that my heart ached right then with pride and love.

"Come here," I said to Char. "You too," I said to Nina. The girls ran over to me and hugged me hard, their little arms encircling me, and I squeezed them back and was happy.

"We need to get that fish back in the water," I said after a little while.

"I can hear it breathing," said Sunny.

"Yeah, it's a beast," I said.

Sunny and I grabbed the carp by its tail and the girls gingerly placed their hands on the sides to steady it, and in this way we moved the fish back into the river, where it paused, waving its fins for a little while before muscling back into the depths.

"Awesome," Nina said. "That was the coolest fish I've ever seen."

"You like that fish, then we really ought to go down to Chicago," I said. "Visit the aquarium down there. Go see some sharks."

The girls returned to the river, splashing more cautiously now, and Sunny and I sprawled out beneath the sun, our fingers brushing and sometimes my own exploring the contours of her ribs, the plane of her stomach.

"They've never called anyone that," she said to me, to the sky. She was serious. "Their real dad left too early."

It was easier for me to tell the girls my own feelings than it was to say in that moment to Sunny that I loved her girls, and that even though we weren't married, I loved them like they were my own, like I *was* their father. So we lay that way, occasionally turning ourselves over or applying lotion or olive oil to each other. Sunny turned the color of walnut wood while my own skin became so pink that in the evening I slept in the bathtub because even the bedsheets of our cool basement encampment felt too warm.

On December first, just before my shift was to begin, and with a blizzard blowing so fiercely that the fire trucks couldn't even leave their garages, there was a fire in the paper plant. The plant burned for three days, flames the height and width of cathedrals licking the gray winter sky. We watched the inferno from our house across the river, and the colors reflected in the water made a second, watery blaze. The front of the house was strangely illuminated for those three days, and the smoke and fumes were so bad that we thought about checking into a motel, but of course there was no money for that, and from the look of things, not likely to be more any time soon.

"What are you going to do now, Daddy?" Nina asked.

I rubbed her hair, tickled her neck; she giggled. "Don't worry about it, kiddo," I said. "We'll be all right. And don't worry about Christmas, either."

"Okay," she said, surveying the destruction across the river, still smoldering, little wisps of gray smoke crawling into the air off the wrecked site.

"Once, in the city of Cleveland, the river caught fire," I said.

"Must have been one nasty river," Nina said.

"The mighty Cuyahoga," I said. "Go get the atlas and find it."

The truth was, I was worried about Christmas. Since summer, things had been as smooth as ever between Sunny and me, almost eerie quiet, and the girls were consistently calling me Dad. I had wanted to organize an extravagant Christmas, but now I had no idea how I'd pull that off. That night I lay in bed with Sunny and said, "I think it might be a light Christmas. Do you think the girls will notice?"

Sunny lay beside me, quiet, gazing at the ceiling.

"Sunny?" I asked, propping myself up on an elbow.

"It'll be okay," she said. "We've always been poor. We never expected anything before, don't expect anything now."

"Are you all right?" I asked. "What's happening? Look, I'm just trying to put my best foot forward here. Trying to make things nice for the girls."

"What? I can't make things nice for my own daughters?" she said, her fighting voice sprung out of nowhere. She reached for her bedside cigarettes and lighted one. I opened the window and the air was bitter cold.

"Shut that fucking window," she snapped.

"Sunny, you know the smoke makes my eyes hurt."

"You want me to go outside?"

"Of course not," I said. "Look, this is our deal, right?"

"Fuck that."

"What's wrong, babe?" I asked.

She was up now, pulling on a pair of tight blue jeans and a low-cut blouse. "Don't worry about it, Dad," she said as she slipped into a pair of cowboy boots. "I'll be back when I'm back."

But she did not come back that night, and I waited until dawn, peering out the frost-latticed windows, watching for headlights or the growl of an approaching motorcycle.

I made pancakes for the girls in the morning and sent them off to school. When they asked where their mother was, I told them she was sleeping. They shouldered their backpacks and shrugged. Sunny frequently slept in on weekends, often until noon. The only oddity was that it was a school day.

After the girls had gone I made a pot of coffee, filled the thermos, and opening the door to go down to the river, barely noticed Geronimo escaping the house.

"Shit! Geronimo!" I cried, running down the street after the cat, but it was too fast and made toward the river and the line of trees at the apex of the riverbank. The cat was well and gone and the day cold. I trod down the bank to the river, and finding a discarded white pickle bucket, sat down heavily as I pulled the flask from my coat pocket.

Great rafts of ice were moving down the full-bellied river, and I remembered my old best friend telling me about a time that he had been fly-fishing at night, with only the light of a full moon. I remembered that he said this was a good time to fish because it was quiet and he could stand in the river in waders and smoke a joint of marijuana without anyone bothering him. He was out fishing with another friend of ours one night when a sheet of ice quietly broke away from shore and clipped the kid at his hips, cutting him in half like a giant sword had just passed through his body.

"I didn't know he was gone," my best friend said. "I was stoned. It was dark. That ice goes down the river without a sound unless it hits something, like other ice. He was gone for hours before I looked up and couldn't find him."

I remember telling my best friend that trains can be that quiet too, especially in winter. That my dad had worked for the railroads and guys were killed every winter because the trains moved so quietly sometimes in the yard in the cold that workers hit by slow-moving trains were just run over before they could so much as scream. No train whistle. Not enough speed to produce a sound or rhythm. Just hundreds of tons of steel moving in a slow, arced line.

I watched the ice flowing down the river and wondered how far it could travel before melting into nothing. I watched the ice move and felt like that full-moon fisherman, his legs taken out from beneath him, dunked underwater and frozen. Sunny was gone, maybe, like I'd known she always would be. And now it was just me and the girls.

The bourbon in the flask tasted good and warm, but there was the feeling that if I kept up drinking, the girls would return from school to find a drunk dad and no mother, so I placed the flask in my pocket and took a sip from the thermos.

Then I stood up, screaming into the empty air, reached into my pocket and threw the silver flask as far as I could out into the river, and it made only an almost inaudible splash. I walked back up the riverbank to my house and telephoned my father, who was happy to hear from me, and I asked whether he might like visitors for Christmas and I told him that the plant had burned to the ground and I had no money for presents and barely enough for the mortgage.

Dad's voice was gruff from the rail yards, from talking over locomotive engines, from the rotation of pipes he kept in a breast pocket of his shirts. "Brucie," he said to me, "get up here and bring those girls with you. How's Sunny?"

"Dad, she's gone, and she left me with the two girls."

"You call the police?" he asked.

"I don't think it's that kind of disappearance."

I heard him exhale deeply. He'd met Sunny only once, at a Fourth of July barbecue, but he had fallen for her hard drinking and he liked that she smoked cigarettes and tolerated his pipe. Late in her teenage years Sunny had been a hobo and rode the rails herself, and she and Dad had talked about that and he was amazed that such a beautiful woman had survived such an odyssey. On my refrigerator under a magnet was a photograph of Dad and Sunny, his arm around her waist, her arm around his shoulder, a cigarette between her lips, his pipe balanced between his teeth and his white and blue conductor's hat happily askew.

"She comes back," he said, "you don't ever let her go again. All right? We'll get her help. Kicking the sauce ain't easy, but it can be done. Your mom and I can come down if we have to."

"Yeah, I don't know that she's ever coming back," I said.

"She will," he said, "she will."

"Dad, I love you."

"Me too, kid," he said. "See you soon."

It was the first winter in memory that the river froze, and I couldn't help but think that all these years it had been the paper plant and its hot excrement that kept the water from freezing. Some days I would stand at the front windows and gaze out at the frozen vein of water and think about my flask and where it was now on its journey down the Mississippi and sometimes I thought about leaving Wisconsin altogether and taking the girls to some point warmer, but there was always the chance that Sunny would come back to a house inhabited by strangers, and that unnerved me as much as the chest of drawers in my bedroom filled with her clothing and lingerie.

I told the girls that their mother was on vacation, which I didn't consider to be an outright lie, because in a way, I told myself, that was exactly what she was doing, what she had done. Vacated the premises.

Christmas had been a success. Dad and Mom bought a pile of presents so vast and tall that it was quickly apparent the girls had never seen anything like it on Christmas morning. There were dolls and clothing and candy and board games and Dad had bought all manner of train paraphernalia, which he told the girls they had to share with their mother.

At one point during Christmas morning Mom was on her hands and knees with the girls, helping them to dress dolls, when Dad patted my shoulder and handed me two presents wrapped in newspaper, which was his signature.

"A little something," he said.

"Dad," I protested, "I didn't get you anything. You didn't have to."

"Shut up and open it."

The first present was a box of Cohiba cigars, and as I examined the markings on the cedar container, it became clear that this particular box had not passed through U.S. Customs.

"Dad, all I smoke is White Owls," I said. "Sometimes Swishers."

"Time for that shit to come to an end," he said. "Open the other one."

It was an old flask, heavily dented, adorned with an engraving of a naked woman in repose. It felt heavy and I shook it: something sloshed inside.

"Maker's," Dad said. "It was full, but you know. Call it a toll sip."

It was strange, I told Dad, that just a few weeks before, I threw the flask my best friend once gave me into the river.

"Don't ever throw this one in any river," he said. "You do and I'll disown you. This was your grandfather's flask from the war." I turned the flask over in my hands, felt its weight. "You don't know about this flask, do you?"

We went down into the basement, where his workshop

was, all his tools hung neatly from pegs on the walls, immaculately spaced and preserved. There were two old recliners down there, chairs my father had used upstairs over the years until they became too stained or threadbare and my mother banished them to this subterranean parlor, where Dad would sit for hours, smoking his pipes and reading Zane Grey.

The flask had belonged to my paternal grandfather, Gus, who had been an Airborne Ranger and had parachuted down over France late in the war. Dodging German artillery, they'd had to alter the plane's flight path such that Gus and his comrades jumped out of the plane over forest heavily entrenched with German infantry, who proceeded to pick them off one by one as they lazily came down to earth, their parachutes so many white mushrooms against the clear blue sky. Gus had seen his friends die, some terribly wounded as they sailed down to the angry earth. Some cut their parachutes off, risking the fall, rather than remain such a slow-moving target. But Gus stayed right as he was, and as he drifted down, he thought about Wisconsin and my grandmother and occasionally nipped off the heavy pewter flask he carried, and sometimes he prayed for protection and sometimes he whistled "Over the Rainbow," but mostly he just enjoyed the ride down, marveled at the patchwork tableau beneath him, the vision of pastoral beauty and wartime horror. Not long before he touched down, still alive, he replaced the flask in his breast pocket, where he was promptly shot, the bullet ricocheting off the metal into a stand of ancient French oak trees. Thereafter Gus traveled everywhere with that flask, carrying it with him even to his job as a high school janitor, where he would sometimes install himself in a broom closet, listening to a transistor radio broadcast baseball games out of Milwaukee as he sat filling the tiny room with cigarette smoke and relishing his brandy or whatever the day's flavor might be.

"It's good luck," Dad said. "Your mom still looks around the lawn for four-leaf clovers, but I don't have the knees for that kind of shit. Besides, you can drink out of this."

He slapped my knee and I hoisted the flask in the air to take my first drink in weeks. It burned of hot metal and fire but tasted like caramel too. Dad extended his hand and we drank like that for a little while, just the two of us, until Mom called from the top of the stairs and we went back up into the light.

"I could use some luck," I said to him.

"Who couldn't?" he said.

By late January, the remnants of the paper mill were no longer smoldering, and I had gotten notice that it would not be rebuilt, that the parent company of the mill was consolidating operations, and that the plant I had bicycled to five days a week had not been profitable even before the accident, would likely never reopen. But a call had come from my old manager Bud, saying that the company had found me another job at another plant, in the panhandle of Florida in a town called Apalachicola.

"It's a promotion," he said. "You'll do what I did up here."

"Bud," I said, "no offense, but mostly you sat at your desk and read *Playboys*."

"Best job I ever had," he said.

I called my dad. "What do you think?" I asked him. "And what about the girls?"

I could hear that he was in his workshop, the low volume of his old transistor radio behind him, the soft scratch of a broom sweeping as he talked, the gentle clinking of tools being put in their place.

"She'll find you," he said. "She'll find you or she'll find us. Either way, you can't turn this down. You got to go. Your mom's ready for a change anyways. She's always talking about those Airstream trailers. Goddamn monstrosities if you ask me, but you know how these things go. My hands are tied."

"Dad," I said, "I can't just leave with the girls. They aren't mine. Not legally."

"Put in the paperwork," he said. "Adopt. I got a friend down there's a judge. Put that paperwork in before you go."

"I miss her," I said to him. "She was bat-shit crazy, but I miss her."

"She'll find you," he said again, and I could picture him nodding his head in confidence. He loved her too.

"I love you, Dad."

"All right, kid," he said. "Keep me in the loop."

The FOR SALE sign was staked into the half slope of our front yard, and I spent the spring painting the house while the girls were in school. It was the happiest time of my life. In the mornings I would burst into their bedrooms, opening the window shades and singing, and they would throw pillows at me, but they always cooperated and it thrilled them that I never told them what to wear or how to do their hair, and I began taking the time to cook hot breakfasts of pancakes and sausages and scrambled eggs and bacon, and before they boarded the bus we would sit around the kitchen table or sometimes on the front stoop and eat together, and they liked to drink my coffee when I wasn't looking, adding huge tablespoons of sugar to my mug. After the girls left, I would drag a radio out onto the lawn and listen to baseball or sometimes old-time rock 'n' roll and I would talk to my neighbors and the neighborhood was a different place during the daytime, a good place, with old people out walking together, holding hands. Or the Hmong fishermen walking toward the river, carrying their buckets and poles and tackle boxes, and sometimes they would stop and show me their catch.

One day, on the ladder, out of the corner of my eye, I saw the sisters as they unfolded themselves from an old sedan and walked toward the back of their house. In one of their hands was Geronimo, looking as forlorn as he had that first night.

"Hey!" I shouted. "Hey! That's my cat! That's my motherfuckin' cat! That's Geronimo!"

I had fairly run down the ladder, dropping a full bucket of paint onto the lawn. Either they couldn't hear me or just pretended not to notice, but they pushed into their dark house just as my feet touched the lawn. I ran across the street and into their backyard, banged on their screen door, my fists warping the frame's cheap aluminum.

"Open up!" I ordered. I banged on the door severely, my knuckles and palms sliced open by holes in the old screen, loose screws. "Open this fucking door and give me my Geronimo!"

A tattered window blind parted and I saw a pair of eyes squinting at me. Heavily wrinkled and bagged, the sunken eyes that stared out at me were red and angry, and I heard one of the sisters croak, "Fuck off." Then the blind collapsed again and there was silence.

"Oh no," I said, realizing perhaps what was about to happen.

My whole life maybe I'd been too meek, and there were times I thought about that and what it had gotten me. It had been enough to work a blue-collar job, dull and anonymous. Enough to lose track of my best friend from high school. Enough to snag Sunny, but not enough to keep her. And there was no guarantee that being who I was would be enough to keep those two little girls in my life. Suddenly I felt a rage, a fury course through me. Fury at the thought that I would watch things be taken from me, that I would fail to fight back.

"Fuck it," I said, and ripped the screen door off its hinges with my bare hands. I heard one of the sisters scream a witchy cry. Then I kicked the shabby wooden back door of their broken-down house with my boot. I kept kicking hard and rhythmically.

"Open that fucking door!" I said. "That's my cat. You hear me!"

The blind parted again, and this time there were two sets of red eyes staring at me, both rimmed in fear. The sisters.

"He's our cat!" they cried. "Our Jerry!"

"Oh, no," I sneered. "The hell he is. Stand back, bitches. Sunny was right about you."

When the girls came home that afternoon, there were police cars parked sloppily along the margins of the street, rooftop cherries ablaze, and I remember waving to the girls as their yellow school bus pulled to a stop in front of our house, all the little faces of its riders pressed up to the foggy windows. They ran to me that afternoon with such desperation and love I might have been Grandpa Gus, coming home from the war. Geronimo was in my hands, and he stunk of neglect, but the girls rubbed their faces against his haggard face and the policeman who was interviewing me even sat down beside me on the stoop and took off his hat.

"Some day, huh?" he said.

"I've had better," I said, my skin itching, my eyes red with allergies.

"We ain't going to charge you," he said.

"For what?" I asked, passing Geronimo into the girls' eager hands.

"Battery, for one," he said. "Breaking and entering, for two. The lesson here evidently is that if you're going to play Dirty Harry, you best accidentally break into a meth lab. You're lucky, is all. The courts normally frown on those types of seizures."

"They had our cat," I said.

The cop took my statement, showed his service revolver to the girls, and then left us on the stoop. Geronimo rolled onto his spine and produced a disgusting stained belly for the girls to rub.

"Inside," I said. "Get that cat to the bathtub now. She's your cat. You clean her up."

The girls raced inside with Geronimo, offering no argument, and I dragged myself over to the refrigerator for a beer. My face was swollen, Geronimo's oil and dander on my skin everywhere. Spring was full on, the air heavy and perfumed with lilacs, on the streets everywhere a dusting of yellow pollen, flowers protruding from the thawed earth, proud as arrows. I sat on the porch and lit a Cohiba with a strip of flaming cedar. I drank my beer and watched the river sashay between its banks. In the kitchen, the girls were bathing Geronimo, giggling, and there was the sound of sudsy water spilling onto the kitchen floor.

The next day the house sold, and weeks later, the bank presented me with a check two digits longer than any I'd ever seen before. The girls and I celebrated by taking a trip to Chicago, to the aquarium, where they were impressed by the sea turtles and sharks and killer whales, though they still talked about my carp and the feel of its leviathan sides against their little fingers, and the awful sound of its giant breathing.

She never came for us, for me, and eventually she became a name that we did not speak, and then, later yet, became like something benign and passing, an epoch of our lives at once sweet and low. The girls sometimes asked about her, but it was with a far-off kind of tone, and I would shrug my shoulders and that was good enough for them. Mom and Dad sold their house in Wisconsin and moved into a nearby trailer court, where they hung Christmas lights shaped like peppers from their Airstream, and in front of the silver bullet of their home was a patch of green turf carpeting, a picnic table, and several chairs, and at nights we would visit them, eat boiled shrimp and drink Budweiser from sweaty aluminum cans.

I bought a blue bedazzled leash for Geronimo, and after dinner we'd walk along the beach with the girls, and they liked the way the cat high-stepped in the sand and fled the very waves he'd just been chasing. My mom would help the girls look for sand dollars while Dad and I loped along behind, swaying sometimes, happy on beer, and occasionally sharing a Cohiba, our pant legs rolled up around our knees, our toes still white from Wisconsin winters, though growing darker every day, and Dad would say, "I think she's still coming, champ. I'm sure of it. Train people, we just move slow." And he would put a hand on my shoulder and I never looked back after that, the salt air good enough for me, the lean and dance of the palmettos something new and exotic, and my little office heavily air-conditioned and issues of a glossy magazine stacking up inside my empty desk drawers.

APPLES

LYLE WAS DIABETIC, and the doctors had already lopped off two of his toes. He moved sometimes unsteadily, but he was a strong man with big hands and most people paid attention to his wide chest and knotty arms. He owned a big smile and rubbed his hands together when he was happy and this made other people happy too; in church on Sundays one might observe the people he greeted almost mimicking his movements, with oversize grins on their shining faces.

He sold appliances his whole life until one day his new boss held a meeting and told the sales staff that they no longer had jobs. There was no fanfare, no pep talk. Everyone walked out to the yellow crosshatched parking lot while behind them the door was locked and the OPEN sign reversed to CLOSED. He went home that day and mowed the lawn. Took greater care with the passes he made using the old red Snapper, the lines in the lawn neat and diagonal. He refilled the birdseed feeders. Cleaned the gutters. When he finished this litany of chores, it was still not even lunch. He stood in the driveway and scratched his head.

Lyle's wife came home that night and he told her the news. It hadn't been a complete surprise. Things had been slow at the store.

"Well," she said, smiling. "You can do whatever you want to now."

He gently rapped his knuckles on the dining room table, making two minor knocks.

She smiled at him and reached over to rub his shoulders, all bone and muscle.

"What do you think you might want to do now?" she asked.

"I've never had to think about it," he replied as he looked at the table. "I've always just had a place to go in the morning."

She reached for his hand and smiled at him as he studied the carpeting, which at that moment looked old, though he had never taken any notice.

His brothers were farmers who worked the land south of town near a village called Strum, and they had work for him, under the table and in cash. They owned some rental properties on the edge of Strum that needed maintenance, so every morning he drove thirty minutes to their small farming town, his truck loaded to the sideboards with saws and tools and scrap lumber.

All of the farms employed Mexicans who lived in the brothers' rentals. Lyle did not speak Spanish. When he entered their apartments, the tenants smiled at him and some of them sat on the beds or at the kitchen tables and watched as he worked. He had always worked with other people and liked having the Mexicans around, even if he couldn't properly commiserate with them.

Sometimes when he was on his hands and knees measuring a piece of lumber, he might point at the back of the truck and say to a small child, "Hammer, por favor." He would make the motion for swinging a hammer. The child would run to the truck and return with his hammer.

"Gracias," he would say to the child.

"You are welcome," they would say. The mothers always smiled at Lyle and sometimes they made him strong instant coffee. Other times they sat in a kind of happy awkward silence and ate hot tortillas and black beans. He would spend those meals concentrating hard to conjure up any Spanish words. Frequently he would end the meal by smiling, bowing his head, and saying, "Gracias." His favorite word in Spanish.

He sat at the kitchen table one night with his wife and they listened to the workings of the old grandfather clock. Their children were gone, scattered around America, and now their evenings were predicated around dinner and television. They liked to fall asleep in front of the blue television, under blankets.

"How are things?" she asked.

"There isn't much left to do," he said. "I'm afraid of being fired by my own brothers."

"Oh, come on, you were not fired," she said, smiling.

"Not yet," he said.

"I mean before. You were just laid off. It happens all the time."

"I know. Basically the same thing in the end, though, isn't it? Either way you don't have a job anymore."

They sat in silence for a while, and he gripped his coffee mug and rubbed his feet against the carpeting. He had very little sensation left in his feet, but he had never told anyone that. He was always afraid of losing more toes. He did not want to be in a wheelchair. Sometimes he had dreams like old reel-to-reel movies in which he was back in his teenage body, with a football in the crook of his arm, running. He woke from those dreams smiling and a little melancholy.

"Are you sad?" his wife asked. Her hair was long and mostly white, but her face was young and full of color.

"No," he said, "I'm not sad. But the thing is, having a job makes you feel important. People need you more. I miss my clients. I miss helping people. I miss feeling important."

"Oh, Lyle," she said, "everyone knows how important

you are." She reached for his knobby hand. The doctors said his hands would grow knobbier and lose some of their cartilage and muscle as he grew older; the diabetes. Sometimes he didn't recognize his own hands or feet.

"Am I still important to you?" he asked her quietly, looking down at the floor.

"Oh, Lyle," she whispered.

She never slept well because she always worried about his diabetic strokes. She did not want to be sleeping if he passed away in the night. He had the episodes about twice a year, and she would awaken to bedsheets soaked in perspiration, her husband delirious, unable to communicate what was wrong. She would run to the telephone to call an ambulance. Then she would run to the refrigerator and pour him a glass of orange juice. She would force him to eat chocolate bars and peanut butter. But she could show no fear, had to be calm for him. They would ride in the ambulance and she would hold his hand as the lights blinked red and blue. He hated that the neighbors might see him being carried away in the ambulance.

She worried almost every day about becoming a widow. They had been married more than thirty years. Sometimes she told the women in her book club that he was like the sun or the moon or the stars to her. It wasn't just that she loved him so much. It was also that he truly seemed to have inhabited her life as long as those celestial bodies had. "How could I get out of bed without him?" she would ask the women of her book club. "How could I fall asleep without Lyle? Why would I eat?" These weren't rhetorical questions. She asked them because she did not have the answers.

His brothers ran out of work for him within three months. He had fixed all the apartments and then moved on to their own houses, where he repaired broken garage doors, window screens, and door locks. He leveled all the refrigerators and checked all of the washing machine hoses and pipes. His brothers' wives pointed at leaking faucets and dead mice. They made him coffee and asked about his retirement.

"Well, I'm not exactly retired," he would say. "Look, I'm right here working."

"Don't you *want* to be retired?" everyone would ask.

"I don't know," he would say. "I've never been."

During the hottest night of the summer Lyle was watching one of his youngest brothers play softball on a baseball field surrounded by corn just outside of Strum. It was adjacent to a bar that sponsored the softball league, and the neon lights of the establishment glowed red and blue like a promise or a reward. Lyle sat in the bleachers with four of his other brothers and they drank pitcher after pitcher of cold, golden beer. It was a familiar beer, a beer that Lyle had drunk in college by the keg, but that night, sitting on the bleachers with his brothers, watching the softball pop so high into the thick August air, the beer tasted better than ever. It tasted like honey. It tasted like butter. It tasted like dandelions. It tasted like summer. The brothers drank pitchers and pitchers of the beer. They took turns walking into the bar for refills, standing in the cold air conditioning, already lonely and excited to rejoin the crowd. They cracked peanuts and threw the shells into the darkness below the bleachers. They watched their youngest brother rope sharp line drives into the outfield. They laughed at him when he stretched a double into a triple and dove headfirst into third base like he was Pete Rose in a gasoline suit. They stood like a small choir to cheer him on until he stood on third base and bowed deeply like a triumphant matador. The other people in the stands burst out laughing too. Everyone knew the brothers.

"This beer tastes *so* damn good," said Lyle.

"It's just the heat, Lyle," said one of his brothers.

"No," said one of Lyle's brothers dramatically. "This beer tastes amazing because this is a special night in America, and I am with my brothers!"

"Sit down, you damn fool," they laughed.

The dramatic brother sat down and drank lustily. On the horizon, zippers of far-off lightning opened the blue and black of the sky.

"Heat lightning," said Lyle.

"No such thing," said one of his brothers.

"So where's the rain?" asked Lyle.

"It's coming," said one of the brothers.

"You can smell it," said another brother.

"Ozone," said a brother.

"Air blowing in from a fresher place," said the dramatic brother.

"Minnesota ain't more fresh," said a brother.

"Air that moves like America," said the dramatic brother.

"Jesus," said his drunk brothers in unison.

The game ended just as a wall of rain hit the field, turning the infield dirt from pale brown to black. The minor assemblage of fans dispersed to vehicles, and the brothers said good-bye and ran crooked routes to their pickup trucks. Lyle was drunk and happy but also feisty. He found his truck and popped on the headlights. He wanted more beer. He did not want the evening to end. He felt young tonight, full of piss and vinegar.

He began the drive home, going slowly. His eyesight was terrible after dark, and the rain that bounced off the steaming hot road made it all the more difficult for Lyle to see the margins of the driving lanes. He hunched over the steering wheel and wiped his forehead and the inside of the windshield, which was quickly steaming up.

Suddenly Lyle noticed he was almost out of gas. He pulled off at a gas station that he knew sold cold beer. He filled his gas tank and the jerry can in the bed of his truck and rushed into the gas station, where the air conditioner made his wet skin tight and cold. He went to the refrigerated wall of coolers and pulled out a six-pack of brown bottles. He approached the register with a fistful of wet dollar bills.

"Sure is wet out there," said the teenage attendant.

Lyle dripped water onto the counter. "And ten dollars of scratch-offs too," he said.

"Sure thing," said the boy as he ripped the tickets off a giant glossy spool. "You must feel lucky tonight."

Lyle paid for the things and, feeling jaunty, opened a bottle of beer right there at the counter as he began scratching off the lottery tickets.

"Ah, mister . . . ," the boy murmured.

"Oh, I'm sorry," said Lyle, feeling invincible and full of beer. "Would you like one too? How rude of me."

The boy blushed, stammered, paused, looked around the abandoned store and surveyed the darkness of the storm outside. "Well, okay," he said. He drank the beer fast, spilling the first sip on his greasy chin, as if determined to down the evidence before it could be used against him.

Lyle finished scratching the tickets and won nothing.

"Bummer," said the boy.

"Story of my life," said Lyle.

"I don't know," said the boy, "you seem like a happy enough guy. Heck, you gave me a beer."

"Well," said Lyle. He looked out at the storm, the water sluicing off the roof and down through the gutters. A single frog hopped across the steaming pavement. Lyle thought: there aren't as many frogs as there once were. "You just never know when your luck is going to run out."

"Work tomorrow?" asked the boy happily.

"Nope," said Lyle, with a sour smile on his face. "Don't have a job anymore." And with that, he left the cold confines of the station and crawled back into the truck. The four bottles of beer sat on the bench seat beside him, jiggling in their cardboard box, a melancholy quartet.

He drove to the store and parked in the empty lot. Inside, the appliances all sat motionless and brand-new: refrigerators and freezers, washers and dryers, stoves and ranges. He opened another beer and thought, *This is what my life was. Machines.* He felt sorry for himself just then. He looked at the jerry can in the bed of the truck full of gasoline. "What the hell," he said. And he went out into the rain.

He went behind the building with his full jerry can, to where the Dumpsters were parked, where he felt no one could see him. "I'm gonna burn this mother to the ground," he slurred. He began lighting matches in the rain, but each one was quickly extinguished. Soon the entire book of matches was soggy and he stood in the rain, still trying to strike the individual matches against the wet book.

"Damnit!" he said.

He grabbed the jerry can and marched back to the truck, sullen and sodden, then drove home.

"There you are," his wife said. "I called your brothers and they said the game was finished over an hour ago. I was worried about you!" Then "Are you drunk?"

"Maybe a little bit," he said. "I was going to burn the store down."

She laughed. "Well, you picked a good night for a fire." She covered her mouth. Her body was shaking with laughter.

"What's so funny?" he slurred, happily now.

"You are the worst arsonist." She giggled.

She peeled off his wet clothes and they made love on the dining room floor, where the carpeting he had thought was old now felt newly wonderful and soft. They fell asleep there for a while and woke up with the final passage of the thunderstorm and its ensuing wet calm. The drip of water off their safe, dry house. They retreated to their bed and slept like two warm embers.

Summer passed just as quickly as it always seemed to, and he moved within his life with a kind of nonchalance that reminded him of high school. He missed his job and the customers that forsook the big-box stores to buy their appliances from him. He missed morning coffee with the other salesmen, and he missed their Thursday nights of beer and cheap cigars. But he was easing into this new life, volunteering more at the church and building furniture in the garage in the evenings.

"Well," his brothers would ask, "are you retired yet?"

"I'm considering becoming a professional golfer," he would joke with a straight face.

"Yeah, on second thought"—they would laugh—"don't quit your day job."

One morning at church Lyle was offered a job. A retired professor who owned a large apple orchard had heard that Lyle had lost his job, and he needed someone to pick the last of the apples from the trees. The orchard was the retired professor's hobby. The bulk of the harvest had already been picked, but there were stragglers on the trees that could be sold for deer bait. He could pay cash and Lyle could keep whatever apples he wanted. Shaking the retired professor's hand, Lyle noticed how soft and elegant it was. How different their lives must have been.

"How will I know what to do?" asked Lyle.

"Oh, you'll figure it out," said the retired professor. "I just need someone I can trust to close the place down before winter. Do whatever you think is right."

"Fair enough," Lyle said.

The seasonal buildings were largely closed when Lyle drove to the orchard; no one was around. His truck was alone in the parking lot. He had brought a small breakfast, a thermos of coffee, and a bagged lunch. For a while he sat on the bench inside the cab of the truck and listened as the old engine ticked away the heat like a steadily slowing metronome. He stared out at the trees in their linear order. He tried to see the last of the season's apples clinging to the craggy branches, but his eyesight was poor. He did not know how long this work would last, and for the first time he wondered how important this job really was. Maybe it was enough that apples fell to the earth and gave the deer and bear and turkey something to eat. Then he shrugged his shoulders and walked into the orchard. If there were no directions and there was no urgency, he would simply create a system for himself.

He started at the back of the orchard and began collecting the apples in empty wooden crates, separating them by quality. He looked for the marks of worms or the birds. He looked for rot. He collected the apples that had fallen to earth in potato sacks. As he worked, he ate a few of the more enticing apples, wasting nothing but the very core.

"Free apples," he said to himself. "All the free apples a man could eat."

By four in the afternoon he had arranged his apples by quality next to the main building and stopped working. He dragged the potato sacks to the side of the building and wrote on a sheet of cardboard: DEER FOOD ONLY. Just then the retired professor pulled into the parking lot in a new black BMW. The foreign automobile was very quiet. Looking over Lyle's work, he smiled.

"You really sorted the hell out of these, didn't you?" he said. "I can probably actually sell some of these crates to the grocery stores. I'll be damned, Lyle!"

Lyle knew the retired professor didn't need any more money. Just the same, he could see that the man was sincerely impressed.

"How long does this work normally last?" Lyle asked.

"I don't know," the retired professor said as he moved some gravel around with a loafered foot. "Until just after frost, I suppose. Or until all the apples are picked. Pray for warm weather, I guess." The retired professor shook Lyle's hand and folded himself back into the BMW. The automobile drove away, with only the tiny sound of gravel against the metal underbelly of the vehicle. Lyle wiped sweat off his forehead, climbed into his truck, and took a bite of an apple.

He liked getting to the orchard early, when there was fog in the valleys and fog hanging like gossamer in the boughs of the little trees. He liked walking around the orchard before he began his work, and sometimes he would sit against the trunk of a particularly old tree and watch as deer moved through the orchard eating the fruit that had fallen in the night. He had never hunted deer. He liked the architecture of their fine legs and their large soft eyes. He liked to watch them bound through the open cornfields, their tails white exclamation marks. He had never told anyone, but he thought their bodies were fragile and beautiful as ornate furniture. The moon was visible still in the morning, and he liked to watch its progress through the sky as the sun rose and the night's fog began to disappear like terrestrial ghosts. He wore a heavy old canvas jacket with deep pockets that he filled with apples that he snacked on all day.

"Don't you get sick of eating apples?" his wife would ask as she washed their nightly dishes.

"Well, he has dozens of kinds," Lyle would reply. "You can eat a different kind of apple every hour all day long."

"I know that, but still . . . you never get tired of apples?"

"They are so sweet," he would reply. "And they're free."

"Do you eat the whole apple or do you just take bites?"

He looked at her incredulously.

"What?" she asked.

"Well, I eat the whole thing, of course. I'm not going to waste an apple. That would be like stealing."

She started laughing.

"What?" he would ask, smiling and rubbing his hands.

"Don't you get full?" she asked, still laughing. Her laughs were full and almost like snorts.

"I *like* apples," he said.

Then they laughed together. They laughed until their stomachs were tight and their faces red.

When he had nearly finished stripping the orchard of its last apples, an old man drove into the parking lot. It was lunchtime and Lyle was sitting in the cab of his truck eating a salami sandwich, listening to the farm report. It was comforting for him to hear the announcer speak the names of different commodities and their prices. Pork bellies. Soybeans. Corn. He liked that these simple things had specific values so important the world needed to be alerted to their constantly fluctuating futures. He wondered what the specific value for a peck of apples was. He watched the old man steadily pull himself from the cab of a very old truck. Lyle left his truck, walked over to shake the man's hand.

"You selling any deer apples?" the old man asked. His voice quivered with age.

"Well, I have about ten tons of deer apples, but I don't

own this place," Lyle said. "I'm just the chief picker and arborist."

The old man laughed and then coughed into a handkerchief.

"All right," the old man said. "Show me what one ton of deer apples looks like."

Lyle walked the old man over to the main building, where dozens of potato sacks full of bruised and damaged apples leaned up against the metal building.

"My *land*," the old man said, "that *is* about ten tons of apples. What would you charge a fella for about three of those sacks there?"

"Tell you what," Lyle said, "pull that old rig of yours over here closer and I won't charge you a thing. I just don't want to drag the damn things too far."

"Sounds like a deal," the old man said.

Lyle loaded the sacks into the bed of the old man's pickup truck, and when he was done he wiped the sweat from his forehead and leaned against the good machine, which was a faded yellow. The same farm report Lyle had been listening to was playing in the man's truck.

"I used to love eating apples," the old man offered.

"I eat about twenty a day," Lyle said. "My wife says I'm going to become an apple."

"We used to have a little orchard when we were first married," the old man said as he looked up at the blue, blue sky utterly free of clouds. "It wasn't much, just about ten trees. You know how many apples ten trees makes?"

Lyle laughed. "Do I ever."

"Ten trees makes about a million apples," the old man said. "You run out of places to put the damn things. You run out of ways to eat the damn things. Applesauce. Apple chutney. Apple salads. Apple cider. Dried apples. I used to hide apples on my wife's side of the bed before she fell asleep. I'd tuck a few in her pillowcase and some down by her feet. Drive her crazy.

"Thing is, in my head, I almost can't remember parts about her. I can hear her voice now and again inside my head, but it's her voice before she died, not when we were young. Not when we were young and had that orchard. I can see her mouth moving, her young mouth, but she's mute. I can't hear anything. Or maybe now I'm deaf, who knows. Hell, I know I'm deaf." He motioned to a huge, antiquated device in his ear.

"How did you meet your wife?" asked Lyle.

The old man scratched the liver spots on his tanned head. He smiled and Lyle saw that his teeth were worn down but still white.

"We grew up together," said the old man. "In the same farming town, near the Mississippi. I always loved her, but I was a coward. I never even spoke to her. We went to the same one-room schoolhouse, the last in the area, two of a student body of twelve, if you can believe it. I sat in the same room as my wife for close to fifteen years and never said a word to her. Just stared at the back of her head and her ankles. I remember that. I remember her ankles now.

"Just before the war started, we were both graduating, and I still hadn't told her how I felt about her, and I probably wouldn't have. I was just going to farm my parents' land, and she was going off to college in Chicago. But then in August, before she was supposed to leave for Chicago, there was the county fair. No one in those days missed the fair, so I met some of my buddies and we bought a bottle and were standing behind a tent getting pretty well soused when I saw her walking through the fair with a younger fellow who had also gone to school with us. And I got so angry! It didn't help that I'd been drinking, but things started to boil inside me. I knew then that I was going to lose her, you see!"

He spat into the dust and gravel and wiped his chin, smiling hugely. Lyle spat too.

"So I followed them. I followed around the fair until they got to that strong man device. That contraption where you hit a plate or what have you with a hammer and it measures your strength. It's a game, you see, and you try to swing that hammer so hard you send a lead weight up into the sky and it sounds a bell for everyone to hear so that people look over and say, 'Boy, he must be strong!' Well, that younger boy took her over to that game and he handed the operator a nickel and he took his swing.

"*Ding!* The son of a bitch hit the bell! Well, I was furious. The operator of the game handed my wife a stuffed animal, and they were about to walk away when I came out of the crowd, drunk, and said, 'I challenge you, sir, to hit that bell more times than I can.' Well, the kid didn't know what was going on. We knew each other from school, of course, and he could probably see that I was drunk, so he agreed. We didn't have that much money, so we decided to swing the hammer five times apiece. And the person who hit the bell the most would win.

"Then the kid turned to me, 'Well, what does the winner get?' he asks. And I looked at my wife and I said, 'The right to escort that young woman home.' Well, the crowd hushed. And then the crowd got loud. Raucous. We rolled our shirt-sleeves up like we were working on the railroad. We unbuttoned our shirts. And we began swinging. After five swings apiece we were tied! That fair sounded like a churchyard on Sunday. That bell was tolling every minute. We did five more swings. Still a tie. The operator of the game stopped taking our money and just watched. Our hands started to bleed. We were lathered in sweat like horses. Little children from the crowd bringing us lemonade. Finally, at swing number forty-four, I beat the son of a gun. He was a good guy too, came to our wedding years later."

"What about your wife?" asked Lyle. "Did you take her home?"

"No." The old man laughed. "She left after the first five swings. Said she was embarrassed and would never be seen leaving a fair with a drunk anyway. Said she was not like a stuffed animal that I could win and take home with me, which of course was right. So the next day I visited her at her family farm, which was where we were married, and we milked cows together and I helped her with her other chores and she told me that I had squandered fifteen years staring at her ankles, because she was in love with me too."

The old man suddenly got very quiet. He sucked a breath of air inside his chest and looked at the immaculate sky.

"I miss her every day like you wouldn't believe," he said. "I used to not believe in heaven or hell or Jesus, but now I do because it's all I got. I got to. I got to see her again somehow."

"That's the best story I've heard in a long while," said Lyle. He lowered his head and kicked the gravel and dust. "That is the best story," he repeated.

They stood in the sun and Lyle admired the old man's yellow truck. The farm report had come to a close and now country music was playing. Lyle did not recognize the singer.

"I'm sorry," the old man said. "I hope that I haven't kept you. Funny to me how things are joined up inside my head. How things just come out. Makes me feel like I'm about to go senile or something. I didn't mean to go on there at the end."

"Don't apologize to me," Lyle said. "Nothing to apologize to anybody about. I appreciate your company. I get so lonely out here sometimes I start talking to the fruit and deer."

"Sure I don't owe you nothing?" the old man asked.

Lyle shook his head. "I wouldn't even know what to charge you. Get a deer for me."

"Oh, I don't shoot deer anymore," the old man said as he slowly climbed into the truck. "I just like to watch them.

They're about my only friends." He shut his driver-side door and drove off.

That night Lyle cut apples. He cut the apples into thin pieces. He tried with clumsy hands to pare the red peels from the apples in single helices with his knife. He put the meat of the apples in an old white bowl that had been his mother's. He added cinnamon and nutmeg and sugar to the bowl of fruit. He even dripped a few drops of whiskey on the fruit. He searched the spice cabinets for vanilla and dribbled some vanilla on the fruit. He folded the apples into a crust and placed the dish in the hot oven that gusted at him with a single wave of heat. He closed the oven and checked his watch. He palmed an apple, walked to their bedroom, and pulling the sheets back, placed the fruit on the mattress, where he knew her feet would later be, then pulled the sheets back, smoothed them just so. He moved back and forth between the kitchen and front door, peering out their windows, looking for her headlights to swing into their driveway. He could not wait to see her.

ACKNOWLEDGMENTS

Infinite thanks to the Iowa Writers' Workshop, where most of these stories were born. In particular, special thanks to James Alan McPherson, who taught me grace, kindness, and decency. To Marcus Burke, whose friendship, cooking, and *hospitality* kept me sane for those two Iowa years. When I had nowhere else to go, the Starlight was always open, and you, my friend, understood what it means *to feel too much*. To Scott Smith, for thousands of rounds of twelve-gauge camaraderie and *civilized* entertainment. And to the rest of the McPherson crew, to Kannan, Christina, Chanda, Adam, Jessica: nobody had more fun than we did. Thanks also to: Sam Chang, Ethan Canin, Michelle Huneven, James Galvin, Connie Brothers, Deb West, Jan Lacina Zenisek, Nicole Neymeyer, David Dowling, Bridget Draxler, and all my other teachers, mentors, colleagues, and fellow workshoppers.

To my agent, Rob McQuilkin, Zorro with a red pen. Thanks for tolerating all these implements of destruction.

To everyone in the Flatiron Building, but in particular my publicist, the marvelous Dori Weintraub, who always found a way to fly me home, even from Georgia—I am in your debt. To my favorite hardworking sales reps, Anne Hellman, Melissa Weisberg, and Tom Leigh: thanks for all that you do. To my buddy Matt Baldacci, who I'll include in this Flatiron list because his friendship transcends time, space, artichoke dip, Budweiser, and war movies: thanks for having my back, amigo. And to Sally Richardson and the late Matthew Shear: long will I remember our *GoodFellas* dinner in the Fedora basement. Thank you for taking a chance on me.

To my mom, Bette Troolin Butler: there you go, Mom, your whole name. To my dad, my wonderful in-laws, all my aunts and uncles and crazy cousins. To my brother (sister), Lump: I love you. To my sister-in-law, Cynthia, for tolerating Lump. To Reidar and Kaitlen.

And to Regina, Henry, and now Nora: I love you bears.